MaTilda

MaTilda

Sarah Gonnet

Holland House

www.hhousebooks.com

Paperback ISBN: 978-1-910688-76-2
Cover design by Katy Smith
Typeset by: Polgarus Studio

Published in the UK

Holland House Books
Holland House
47 Greenham Road
Newbury, Berkshire
RG14 7HY
United Kingdom

www.hhousebooks.com

To Emma Gonnet, you make my work possible

PART ONE

TILDA

I'm not here.

There's blue paper over my stomach. I should have shaved my legs, they're thick with stubble. The doctor is standing rubbing Vaseline onto his plastic device. His fingers slip over it a bit and knock it open.

I'm not here so I didn't just see how wide that thing can go.

I count my pain on my fingers as he slowly pushes it inwards.

"One, two, three, four."

The counting is something my mother taught me. She always claimed she got through childbirth without painkillers but one day, when The Problem was just beginning to raise its head, my dad took me aside and told me otherwise. Told me she had had an epidural. Since then when too much wine at family dinners have made her tell the story again, I have never let on that I know. Her pride is bound to that pain.

He makes one last push and I almost shout the numbers aloud.

"One

"Two

"Three

"Four."

I inhale the clinical air. Over my knees I can just make out his metal tray of objects. He picks something long and thin.

I hear the pop of a packet opening. Then I feel a scratching inside me. I think he's put a cotton bud up there. One of those with a really long stem. A second cotton bud follows. Then he pulls the plastic out of me, making my eyes water.

"Thanks." I cough, thinking that he's done.

"Just one last pull. It's got a bit stuck."

He yanks at the speculum again and it feels like he is taking my insides with it.

"Fuck," I mutter and then, "Sorry." Are you supposed to swear in front of doctors?

I sit up cautiously. My insides throb.

"We'll have the results back in a week or so. Ten days at the most," he says and doesn't look up at me again as he begins to label the parts of me that he has taken.

I squeeze my knees back together. When I slide myself off the bed my feet plop back into my ballerina pumps.

Once the doctor indicates I am free to escape, I walk back down the corridor to the waiting room; then beyond to outside, with a distinct lack of ballerina grace.

Our house stinks of coffee. I make mine black even though David frowns at me. It's the usual, a frown that says I need to put some weight on. He tinkles the blue capped milk carton at me but I turn away from him, towards the TV. He doesn't ask me about the appointment. I can't blame him entirely, we both thought it was only a rash. He still could have asked though.

"Toast?"

I hate that he's become my monitor.

The TV tells me there been a murder, an earthquake, three sexual assaults on underage—

"Cereal?"

Shaking my head I leave the room, go upstairs and sit on the toilet. I stay in there for an abnormally long time because I want him to think I'm throwing up. Whilst I'm there I have a look in my pants. There is a light spotting of blood but nothing worth putting a sanitary towel on for.

Eventually I carefully creep out and downstairs. I try to pull my bag down quietly from the peg on the cupboard, but the door creaks and he's on me.

"I'm going to college."

"You got money for lunch?"

"I'm not a kid."

He tries to give me a cereal bar. I leave without it.

"I know you're not a kid!" he shouts after me.

I don't turn around.

I'm sitting in college with my feet flat against the fake whitewashed wall that marks out the boundaries of my tiny studio space. I draw something but nothing that could be construed as work. It's some kind of creature from a corner of my brain. My battered oil pastels scratch away at the paper and end up satisfying some emotional itch. I sketch out a wide anime eye with scrawny, towering legs. I work around it too, quickly making a mountainous landscape and twisted orchids emerging from the ground. Before I'm done I realise the eye is staring me out and I turn the page on it. I like beginning again anyway.

Everyone else is in the workshop room for registration. I've missed it and I don't care. They're all kids anyway, straight from school. Being a mature student makes me seem elderly to them. And their fucking giggling…

It takes determination to enter the dingy toilets that service the entire art department. Once inside I head for the first cubicle I see. I'm hit by a new, fishy, smell and sure enough there is a throbbing red tampon in the toilet bowl. I try to sit down and ignore it, but I can't. So I back out again, and look around, but I'm forced to realise it's the only cubicle free.

I really need to go.

I enter again, sneaking up on it, as if that will make a difference. I give the flush button a hefty push but it bobs up to the top again.

The movement of the water dilutes some of the blood from the main mass.

I should pick it up and put it in the bin.

Remember that time dad pulled a decapitated mouse out of a trap and it bled everywhere, all down his arm?

I back out again, deciding I'll pee on the floor if I have to.

Just in time a girl in full cosplay (cat ears, Alice in Wonderland dress) backs out of another cubicle and I make a run for it.

I'm back home on our battered sofa. The TV blinks to offer me soaps or soaps or the Mystery Channel. There was no money for Sky Atlantic this year and my usual torrent sites are down. I need to see *Game of Thrones*, I'm months behind (and *Penny Dreadful* but I don't as freely admit I like that one. Secretly I wish I was a witch drawing pentacles in salt).

Instead I'm sat here watching ancient episodes of *The Bill*.

They're not even in chronological order.

Some of the ad-breaks dissect lines of the script down the middle.

TV off and music on. First up on the playlist is Courtney Barnett. The sound makes me limp along instead of dancing, like a cowboy in a western who's been shot in the leg: I have bursts of energy but ultimately I trip myself up.

I should be drawing. My sketchbook is gaping wide and white on the sofa behind me. The sofa isn't as clean as the pages. It's covered in paint and tactless throws of varying shades of orange.

The tampon.

I keep seeing the tampon like a horror-film flash.

I need a wee but I don't dare go. I'm going to see it, and then the blood and then the blood will bubble up out of the bowl and then…

The garden?

It would be an option, except there are those loose planks in the fence and I'm fairly sure Mia, the neighbour, can see through it. It's certainly big enough for me to collect all the tab butts up and drop them through when Mother visits.

David will be home soon.

I should be drawing.

I should cook him a meal. Or order in.

Order in. I'll just have a couple of his chips and claim I already ate.

I should be drawing.

I really should be drawing.

He comes home and switches the music off. It had shifted to Laura Marling and he hates Laura Marling.

I haven't cooked dinner.

I haven't ordered in.

I try to suggest this to him with my eyes, but he insists on looking in the oven anyway.

"It's not even on." I say and then go upstairs to sit on my own again. He shouts something after me that I pretend so hard to ignore I forget to actually listen.

I try to go back to the TV but it's the time of day when quiz shows take over and I can't handle them. They always get to me because of their intense music. Music that is always counting down to something. Counting down whilst the viewers waste their lives. Not something I have anything against, but there is no point in emphasizing it. I just can't do all that so I go to bed instead. It's only five in the afternoon but I drop off straightaway.

I wake up with one of the mattress springs driven hard into the small of my back. In my half-conscious state it makes me think of a penis. An old memory of a hard penis from when I was in high school. David is so stressed by the whole training to be a doctor thing that he can't quite get there. Not that I particularly care. I'm not as driven as I used to be either.

I go back to sleep.

I wake to him snoring.

I get up, get my notebook and try to write.

My brain spits out two paragraphs, then leaves my pen wavering over the rest of the blank page. I get Robin Thicke lyrics in my head, maybe because of the mattress spring; maybe because I want to be a feminist but my brain thinks I'm an idiot.

I write out *Blurred Lines* for the rest of the page. Then I cross it out, blurring the lines with thick pen.

I should tear the page out, but I don't want to ruin the sacrament of the notebook. Every word is sacred.

Shit. Just like that *Every Sperm is Sacred* is in my head.

I spend the rest of the night watching Monty Python sketches on Youtube. My mother used to love Monty Python. She could do all the voices and memorised whole scenes of the films. Then she'd just come out with them when we were sat in a café or something. Locally they got used to the Spam song being sung at every opportunity, but when we went to Paris one summer she got spat at. It made her start smoking again. Over there they have multi-coloured Ladies' cigarettes. I begged for a puff because I thought they were fruit flavoured. Eventually she gave in and let me hungrily suck the smoke up. I almost choked.

I wake up again. He must have come and gone during the night. I gently fondle the indent in the mattress where he was.

It's easier to love him when he isn't there. I'll give him some credit though, he didn't wake me up when he got up this morning. I hold this thought until I go into the kitchen and find ten thousand pans in the sink from the hefty breakfast he evidently cooked for himself. Then I open the locked cupboard (where he insists we keep household products because that's how his mother did it at home) to get the washing up liquid, and find a prominently placed ClearBlue test. Is he poking holes into our condoms?

I walk away from the cupboard and leave the kitchen a mess.

A new morning. Not particularly bright. Not the apocalypse either. Should I go into college today? It's become a regular question now. I used to love art. I used the word "passionate" six times in the personal statement I attached to my UCAS application.

But today to get in I'd have to: have a shower, get dressed whilst wet, put some make-up on, rub make-up off, re-do make-up, re-do make-up again, pack my bag, find my fucking keys, walk up to the bus stop, wait up to an hour for the bus…

Sitting beneath the narrow set of shelves and drawers David once built for my make-up, I paint my nails, all the time trying to focus on the middles and not perfecting the edges. Perfectionism in nail painting only leads to bumpy slips of polish. I've chosen teal for one hand and sparkly blue for the other (odd hands, odd socks, odd Converse). I don't think that reflects anything about what I'm feeling, but you never know.

The doorbell rings and its Mia. I can tell from the prim perfection of her push.

I open the door and say "Sorry, I'm just in the middle of something." and let her make her own way in.

Mia sits down and then I sit down.

I nervously blow on my nails because I wish I could do my cardigan up to hide my stomach flab.

"Hello Tilda. I was wondering how you were getting on."

"With what?"

"College. You're still at college aren't you?"

"Yeah. I started again, got fed up with English Lit half-way through second year. It's uni really. They just call it college because it's an art school."

"So they call it school?"

"No. They call it college. You were right."

She looks impressed with herself.

"Whatever. I never claimed to know all about these things."

"Well it's a university course but—"

I stop. Mia is looking at her watch; she isn't listening to me.

"I would stay and have a chat, but to be honest I came here to ask a favour."

"Really?"

"Yes. Just a small one and I'll pay you of course. Give you some extra money for paintbrushes or something."

I want to throw her out, but money is money.

"Ok."

"Could you watch Jason for a few hours? His Au Pair is sick and I need to go out."

His "Au Pair"?

"Business dinner," she clarifies.

I nod, try to get over… His"Au Pair"?

"Yeah sure."

I never even knew she had a kid. Where does she keep it? I've never seen it.

"Thanks. I'll send him round in half an hour. I'll pack something for his dinner, he's very fussy."

"I'm doing pizza—"

"He really is very fussy."

I lead her out of the door, touching my nails against her pale M&S coat and staining it with teal strands. She won't notice straightaway, but it's the kind of thing her bitchy friends will probably point out when she meets up with them.

The kid comes round with a Tupperware box full of salad.

"Hey I'm Tilda." I say and bend down to shake his sticky hand. "You like pizza?" I ask and he nods violently. "Good."

I haven't got any toys so I give him one of the boxes we shoved in the spare room when we moved in, telling him it's a ship.

Then I go and smoke in the next room. Something about the sight of a kid apparently makes me want to smoke. Plus I'll need all the hunger-suppressing effects possible to deny myself a full pizza later. When I was a kid we'd have it as a takeaway all the time. I'd finish mine dead quick then guzzle down any left-overs as well. I was disgusting.

Cigarette finished I check on the kid again and then order a pizza. I'll just sneak a couple of slices from his. David won't be home until after we're done. Most kids eat at about five yeah?

He likes the box, which is good because it means I can watch TV. I shove on a boxset of *The Following* then remember that he's only seven and stick on *Mad Men* instead. If a kid was going to drink they'd probably go for alcopops not bourbon so I'm probably safe…

…I wake up to next door's cat mewing.

In a panic I check the kid, but he's fine, asleep on the other sofa.

David opens the door. Evidently the mewing had been because he had been approaching.

"Something smells nice. Who's the kid?"

"Its Mia's."

At some point the pizza must have arrived.

David opens the box.

"You didn't get me anything?"

"The kid ate it all," I say.

"For fuck's sake Tilda! I'm hungry."

"So are the hippos."

"What?"

"Hungry, hungry hippos."

"What the fuck does that mean?"

I bite the air next to his face, just like a hungry hippo.

He walks off back into the kitchen and starts to heat up a tin of curry.

"Do you really think…" he starts to say as it comes to boil.

"What?"

"Nothing."

"What?"

"How many times have I suggested we…and you say…"

"What?"

"You say you're not ready…and then you take in someone else's…"

"Yeah, for one night. That's not the same thing."

"Yesterday you wouldn't even let me talk about kids."

"So?"

"Nothing. Stir this. I'll check on him."

I stir the curry but I don't touch the bottom with the spoon so that there'll be a burnt layer for him to wash up.

I almost knock it off the hob and all over myself when David wails from the next room.

"Fuck! Tilda! Fuck!"

"What now?"

"Call an ambulance."

"Why?"

"The kid. The fucking kid Tilda. He's barely breathing!"

"What?" I refuse to move, so he comes in and drags me through to the other room.

"Look!"

Clutched in one of Jason's hands are the innards of a pill-packet.

That's right. I took some sleeping pills.

I gave him the packet. He was popping it like bubble-wrap.

Was the packet empty?

I'm sure the packet was empty.

"It was empty. We were playing a game."

"Phone a sodding ambulance."

David is right there clearing Jason's throat and checking his pulse.

"Call. The. Ambulance."

"It was empty."

I dial.

MATILDA

August 8th 2015

Hey,

Is that the right way to start a diary? "Dear Diary" seems a little too formal. Should I give you a name, like Anne Frank did? The looming mythical diary reader. Do you read everyone's diaries? Or just mine?

Today I watched *Gone With the Wind.* I still have that battered VHS copy mum bought me as a kid. And the DVD I bought as a teenager with newspaper round money. And two re-mastered copies. The one I watched today was the HD DVD version. Blu-ray seems like a bit of a rip-off. What do you think? Or are you from the future? I wonder if they'll do a 3D version.

I love all the colours of the sunsets and the land, but mostly I enjoy watching for subtle signs of Vivien Leigh's illness. I like trying to pick up whether she was manic or depressed when they filmed each scene. It's mostly in her lips and her eyes. Her eyes lag behind her mouth when she's depressed and of course her mouth races when she's manic, but not as fast as her eyes. Sometimes I watch *Jeeves and Wooster* and do the same for Stephen Fry. Their facial expressions are eerily similar in places.

I'm guessing you can tell I'm between jobs right now. Yet

somehow I'm fairly calm about it all. It should be obvious because in times of stress I forget about Vivien and Marilyn and the others and turn to *Mad Men*. No plot, gentle jokes, smooth jazz and constant irony just have a way of easing my mind. I think it has something to do with Jon Hamm's voice as well.

Actually, thinking about it, I do quite want to watch *Mad Men*. Specifically the episode where Betty shoots at the doves. It's one of my favourites. I've always wanted to hold a gun. I joke sometimes that if I had any discipline I would have joined the army.

Maybe I should go back to uni and turn my fashion FdA into a BA. I couldn't go back to Glasgow, obviously, but I could do something locally. They would probably let me have a loan. If I begged. (Is this tone alright for you? Or do you find chatty annoying? The only diary I've ever read is Anne Frank's; and that one is pretty grim, for obvious reasons. We read it at school. It was better than when we learnt about World War One. The teacher I had that year just made us watch all of *Blackadder Goes Fourth*.)

(Oh, and Marilyn Monroe's but I'm not sure she even wrote that.)

My tits hurt. It's been happening a lot recently. A kind of ache. I've checked, no lumps. Though apparently if its cancer the lumps don't hurt anyway.

At first.

Fuck. Sorry. That did get dark. I'm going to put *Mad Men* on now. Maybe that will even me out a bit.

Watching this is starting to give me ideas. I should learn how Joan's outfits are constructed so she doesn't look fat. I could do with some of that. I haven't made my own clothes since I was a teenager. Even during the course. They would always make you create stuff to fit a size 6 model. I'd rather not tell you what I look like. Then you're free to imagine whatever you want.

Maybe I should learn to read the tarot cards my mum bought me. She's currently having her second New Age crisis. The first was in the seventies before I was even born, but I've seen the photos.

It would be nice to have the skills of a Wise Woman.

Maybe people would even pay me for it.

Carnival tarot reader, a more reliable job than journalism.

I need a bath. My boobs are stabbing me as if they're growing. I hope it's just hormonal. I used to get this all the time when I was a teenager. My mother would say I'm getting fat (I call her Mother whenever she references my weight). They can't be growing now though? Can they? I'd say I could be pregnant, but you can't get pregnant without the sex bit.

The noise of the taps emptying themselves is vaguely soothing, like I'm going to immerse myself in a ditch dug with a pneumatic drill, but in a good way. Still, I should probably get a plumber in.

Still soggy, sorry about the drips! I'm just logging onto my computer… writing with one hand…So yeah… I can't shield you from this… I suppose online dating isn't for everyone, but then there's that afternoon when you're bored and lonely and you find yourself staring at a screen.

I'm probably not going to show up for any of them; but there's this one guy who looks perfect. Not perfectly "perfect", because I don't like "perfect" but he looks like what I want. It might just be that thing where the estate agent shows you an amazing set of photos of a flat and then you see the actual thing and it has rising damp and broken central heating, and then the boiler explodes whilst you're on the tour.

Maybe I will go. It's not like I'm going to meet anyone in any other way. Unless I get a job. This is much less daunting than all that.

I replied.

I committed.

I booked.

Short sentences.

Dramatic emphasis.

My life is a thriller.

It's all done and I'm watching *Six Feet Under* on boxset. I like Clare now she's at art school, still can't get along with Nate though. I'm seeing the guy tomorrow.

It's been decided.

I have to go.

So… here I am, sitting in the restaurant we agreed on, trying not to gulp down wine even though my tongue is dry. He isn't late,

I'm early, but somehow it seems like he's already on the clock. I could get my book out and read a biography of Yves Saint Laurent I found in a charity shop yesterday. I still make my own bags, which means that they're all built to hold a book. This one is felted and in the shape of a strawberry. I love the slow scraping of the felting process. I picked the strawberry one because I wanted to be carrying something memorable in case he is tricked by my plain face into quickly forgetting me.

Now he is late. Two minutes… but still late.

I switch on my iphone and watch a YouTube video of Ida Ekblad preparing to sculpt by tossing wrought iron scraps down an enormous tower of metal.

Yves Saint Laurent by Alice Rawsthorn. Yes, I've finally decided to just get my book out. I don't read the pages of books in chronological order. I never have. Instead I flick through until I find a page that fits my mood and read on from there. I can tell what I have already read because I draw and make notes all over the pages. Somehow books make more sense to me like that. Palimpsests.

I'm getting weird looks from the waitresses though. Some people think books shouldn't be tampered with.

Yves Saint Laurent continued designing couture from his room in a mental hospital. I gave up when I broke up with my first long-term boyfriend.

Shit.

He's here.

Warning: this is a post-coital entry. I'm sat on the loo, but I've washed my hands so this is probably still a low germ risk. Could germs survive from my time until yours anyway? Or would they just multiply and colonise these pages? Mutating into the bacteria that finally wipes the world of human life?

"There's a hole in it." he said to me, maybe half-way there.

"Oh fuck."

That's when he reaches down and fiddles.

"I think it's ok."

"It isn't."

He goes back down; brushes his hands on me. Evidently he decides it has split because he sighs an "Ok" and rolls off me, to one side.

"Do you have another?"

"No. That was my last."

He leaves the room. Then I hear the stairs creak and the front door bash closed. I roll over and try to finish it myself but I quickly give up and get my book back out.

But that's not the end… Aha! A twist! What tension!

It's four in the morning. The doorbell goes.

It goes again.

And again, with more anxiety, a longer buzz.

I anxiously go to it. It's him. I open the door.

"Supplies!" he shouts and throws three boxes of condoms at me. "All the pharmacies were shut and I didn't trust the ones at the corner shop so I ran home and got some! Only ten miles!"

I let him in. I think I like him.

"What's your name?" I ask.

"Thomas."

MOTHER

The slowness starts in my fingers. Then my calves seize up and I almost drop.

That's what people don't get. It's a physical thing. It's not just in my head. It spreads much further than that. All I do feel in my head is a coldness. It's like when you get chilled to the bones and can't warm up even if you sit against a radiator. Except it's deep in my brain, not my bones. I feel something else in my bones. An itchiness.

I don't like the word "depression."

TILDA

I'm staring into space, examining the slight stain growing out and up from the skirting board. Then my dad is there, sat opposite me. He is talking and I'm not listening. But then I never listened to my parents properly so I don't think they can tell the difference. He keeps on talking anyway.

David's home from work, but he's in his room playing games, where he can smoke without them knowing. I'm going to order food for the two of us later. It's part of the routine now, although he is trying to get me back on to cooking microwave meals.

I wish my dad would leave. I catch snippets of what he's saying, and it's as if he and David are both talking out of the same mouth.

"Tilda…You were very lucky… I seriously… you should… you need… no I just feel that… he nearly…Tilda. Tilda. Come on…you have to see that…You can't just…a therapist… medication… we can't… come on…"

I get up and walk out.

As a kid I used to run away from home all the time. Now I walk.

6

6.30

8

9

9.03…9.05…9.10…9.11…9.15…9.18…

Tonight I won't let myself go to bed before ten.

The doctor won't give me any more sleeping pills. I shouldn't have asked directly, I should have just subtly suggested it… I must have come off as an addict.

The police should phone tomorrow.

The lawyer said it should be ok. The kid only inhaled the dust of the pills… or licked the packet. They think he may have licked the packet…

I can't remember if there was a pill left.

He was only unconscious. Probably asleep.

I can't remember if there was a pill left.

It should be ok.

It should be ok.

Unless they come and arrest me.

Dust. Its dust. It was…

"The kid didn't even die Tilda. Don't be like this."

I'm already in the bed. He is at the sink re-washing his hands. I curl my legs in so that even if he goes for me he won't reach anything much. He swings his thighs in behind me, and folds his body around mine. His hands wander but my plan works. Within ten minutes he is snoring behind me. I wriggle away and put my headphones in. I eventually fall asleep at three in the morning listening to *Glitch Mob* and having brief, trippy dreams.

Then I wake up at five and make coffee.

And it's back.

Dust? *Dust?* Did I leave… was there a pill…?

I try to picture the packet when I gave it to him. Was all the silver scraped away? Was there a crevice still plump with a pill? I can't… I can't…

Did I do this?

And if I did… does that mean I should never have children… could never be trusted with… I'm not ready now, but what… what if I'm never ready?

When the phone rang I thought it was the police, but it was college. I haven't been in for two weeks. When did two weeks happen?

They want to know why.

I shout at them. I shout that I almost killed a kid because I was so off my face because my life is so shit and my brain moves around in my head as if I'm not a real person at all that my brain is a barfing bubbling monster blasting out bubbles made of pieces of brain, bubbles blown through blood out into the world like one of those kid's electric bubble machines— oh and I probably left a pill in the packet.

Fucking dust. Complete bollocks.

I don't think I'll be going back to college.

I can't afford it, but Starbucks does the biggest cups of coffee out of all the chains, so I can sit there and nurse it for longer. I don't dare go out to smoke in case they clear the table while

I'm gone. So I'm stuck, sat in Starbucks, sipping foam and staring into space. A couple of times, while I'm sat there, I hear the noise of an ambulance approaching, only for it to never pass by.

There's a man sat outside handing out leaflets. He's talking to himself. I want to go sit with him.

I got a letter through from the doctors today. I've got it in my bag. I haven't opened it. I'm not going to open it.

MATILDA

11th August 2015

Hey Diary!

He's a poet. Seriously.

Fuck. He's a poet.

Literally a poet.

I picked up a fucking poet.

Maybe he made it up?

But he'd already pulled me so…

Yeah, yeah, the sex is good/average.

Oh— and we're going to Copenhagen. He told me last night.

14th August 2015

Hey again,

We're on the plane. I even love the way he says.

"I need the loo."

Which is fortunate as it's the third time in half an hour. I think he might be scared of flying. I can't quite bring myself to ask him and he isn't volunteering any information. I totally wouldn't care about it if he told me… but then, he doesn't know that. He's changed a bit since the euphoric planning stage. I hope it's just while we're in the air. I've stood up to let him past every time he needs the loo and he hasn't once attempted to touch my arse. Very unlike him. I think. I can't claim to really know him yet, I suppose.

Ah, he's back and he's just told me that I'm going to *love* Copenhagen. Again. At least seeing a new place will give us something to talk about. I'm going to stop writing this and get us both a drink. Maybe that will help the flow of the conversation.

You don't think this is all too quick? Do you?

15th August 2015

Hey,

We're at the house and (he's borrowed it from a friend so I can't really blame him) it is yellow. Like Van Gogh and Gaugin's Yellow House. YELLOW. He's going to write so he gets the room with the biggest window, but mine still looks out over the patch countryside this house guards. Yes… we're in separate rooms. My mum would be proud.

Oh dear reader, I worry I've made a mistake.

I would tell you about today but I've got that weird thing before a migraine, where people's faces look like Picasso pictures or mismatched jigsaws. I tried to describe it to Thomas like that and he accused me of being a cliché. That seems to be his ultimate insult.

"Cliché bitch!"

I actually made that up. He has never said that to me. I actually can't imagine him using the word "bitch".

I was really hoping this trip would be more exciting. Don't stop reading yet. It could be just around the corner.

He's out. I'm jacking someone's internet to watch Hannibal fan videos. I have the volume up way too loud, so that there is basically no point is wearing the headphones, I'd be able to hear it fine without them on. Instead I'm forced to admit that I quite like the tingles of pain on my eardrum; and the fact that when I emerge from this musical bed-cave I'm going to be partly deaf.

17th August 2015

Today he took me to the Royal Theatre. Not to see a performance or anything, just to take a look around. It was all gold paint and chandeliers. But I spent most of the time we were there examining the busts that were all over the place. They didn't have eyes, just holes, like when someone donates their organs and they're buried with no eyes (not something I've personally seen but something I imagine weirdly often). I tried to work each one out. They were all probably composers or playwrights, but in my head they became fishmongers with cheating wives; Tesco slave stackers with degrees in Astrophysics; greengrocers who want to be chefs, but don't have an oven- just a microwave— Do they even have Tesco here? We've been doing all out shopping at outdoor markets, like in a rom-com.

Alone again. He's out "writing" in cafes, so I'm going to take this opportunity to get a look at that view in his room. I slide a couple of paintbrushes down the pocket of my men's jeans (men's jeans have much better pockets) and pull my painting t-shirt on over my head. At home I usually work in a partially destroyed pair of dungarees, but if I'd packed them the paint and oil and acrylic filler would have rubbed off on my other clothes. Armed with my sketch pad and watercolour box I push through the forbidden door, into his room. He hasn't let me in yet. Obviously we've slept together, but it's always in my bed.

There are books and papers and scratty notebooks everywhere. He packed a huge litre rucksack to get here and I doubt there was any room for clothes with this lot. Some of the books are in Danish so he must have bought then since we arrived. He seems to be good at picking up the language but I didn't realise he was good enough to read a book in it. I half want to start tidying, sorting, making this mess make sense— but I can't let him know I've been in here. I'm not entirely sure how he would react.

Trying not to breathe in the smell mouldering coffee, I pull back the huge grey wings of the curtains. Light slides inside and I begin to paint.

MOTHER

When you close your eyes do you see lights? Flickers and shadows suggesting shapes?

I do.

I play this game where I press gently on my eyes when they're closed. It lets you control the shapes. Maybe make pictures.

I can't write today.

I have an idea, I start writing it, and then before I finish one line, it disappears.

Then I get another idea and another, but nothing endures.

Nothing sticks.

I can't end, I can only begin.

Nothing is neat.

Nothing is complete.

TILDA

"Nothing."

He wants to know what I did all day.

"Nothing?" he asks.

"Nothing." I say.

Then we sit in silence until he switches the TV on.

"Anything for dinner?"

I shrug.

He goes into the kitchen and returns with a tin of pinapples. He pulls the tin open by the ring rather than using the tin opener. I almost shout at him that I'll cut myself washing it up later…then I remember I don't wash up any more.

I sit some more.

I realise he is talking to me.

"What?"

"Have you eaten at all today?"

They finally gave me sleeping pills again. A tiny dose, but I can bulk them up myself by using the "I lost the first lot" double order technique. It's good to sleep when you're not eating. Not that I have hunger to sleep through. I could eat. I totally could eat. The fact is I'm just not hungry. And I'm still alive aren't I? Three meals a day is a bullshit rule created by society. Really you don't need to eat much more than twice a week. It's worked for me. Although I'm not actually losing as much weight as I would like. In fact, every day I seem to be getting fatter. I can't face getting on the scales. I think he's hidden them.

"You don't sleep."

"You don't eat."

"You sit there the whole time and stare into space. What part of that sounds like you're ok?"

There is nothing but space around me. Nothing but nothing.

"I'm fine."

"I can see your bones Tilda."

"Good," I mutter.

"What?"

"Good," I shout.

"You're going to die. You have to stop punishing yourself for something that never even happened," he says.

"But it did happen. I fucked up so bad."

"It could have been worse."

I make this…noise…I can't help it.

"You need to make a new start. We could move away," he says.

I'm gulping for air like he's just kicked me out of my fishbowl.

"What? Things need to change," he says.

I stand up. I sit down. I'm not going to run.

"My dad." It's a suggestion that pains me, but a suggestion I have to make.

"Your dad hates me! And he's hardly any good for you—"

"At least he tries to care about me!"

"I am trying. You're making it fucking impossible. Why do you do that?"

"I'm cursed," I say.

"Shut the hell up. You can't get out of this with…with… faux paranoia," he says.

I stand up. I've changed my mind. I'm going to run.

Then I see black, with multi-coloured specks.

There is a deafening hum.

"You fainted," he shouts at me.

Why is he shouting at me?

"I've called an ambulance," he says.

"No…" I begin to say.

"Yes Tilda," he says.

"No!"

I try to stand, but I can barely move my legs.

"I'm terrified Tilda."

I want to scream in his face.

I can't even open my mouth.

MOTHER

Sometimes I feel like I have two children.

MATILDA

21st August 2015

Hey there,

Reading "My Story", supposedly by Marilyn Monroe (ghostwritten by Ben Hecht), for probably the four-hundredth time. Her childhood doesn't compare much to mine. I sincerely hope that suffering is not a precedent for creativity; though this extended fallow phase I've been going through since college seems to suggest otherwise! I thought maybe spending time with a poet might help; but now the holiday is over and I just feel…

…I'm not sure I'm going to see him again… although I do still have the remains of his condom collection.

Fuck. I just read that back- I wrote "precedent" and "fallow" in the same sentence. His love of words is rubbing off on me. Is that a good thing? Or is it bad? Will I completely lose my identity if I stay with him? Anyway, it isn't precedent. Prerequisite?

There was this note on the doorstep. It must have been dropped off whilst I was still asleep.

Matilda,

Please!

And I'm sorry. Phone me.

No name but then I don't need one.

Another note appeared this morning, before the postman, before I'd even set off for my jog.

Matilda. Matilda. Matilda.

Do you remember where we first met?

I'm waiting for you.

We only met four weeks ago! And I suppose he means where we first met physically (in that dive of a bar) not on the internet.

I log into my computer. Fourteen emails of one word "Matilda". He's officially stalking me now.

But he's a gentle stalker.

Maybe I could just see him once? For closure…

…or maybe not. I just looked out the window and he's outside my house, staring up. I'm trying not to look at him again. I shouldn't encourage him.

He's cute though, like a puppy. Not that I'm a massive fan of puppies.

I can't sleep. Not because he's creeping me out. He's not creeping me out. Surely this should be creeping me out? Who am I?

It's morning and he's still there. I'm ready for my run. He must be freezing.

I kneel down and lift the letterbox flap so I can see through it. I stare at him for a while. He barely moves the whole time. He just occasionally shifts his weight from one foot to the other. Has he been doing that all night? He must have sat down for a while at some point. Surely? He looks like one of those street performance statues. Should I go out? Everything I know about stalkers, drawn from a boxset of *Criminal Minds,* is telling me no.

I'm sat in the kitchen. The window in here is out to the back. I'm continuing "My Story"; the chapter called "Up and Down Again". It's the one with the photo of Monroe wearing a patched, flowing skirt. I stare at the picture for much longer than I consider the words. Her face is so expressive but her hands tell me more. I always like to guess things about people from the way they hold their hands. Her hands are vulnerable.

I go back to the skirt. I could make a skirt like that. I plan the pattern in my head, then pick up an old, stubby pencil and sketch the design in the corner of the page. I need to go to a charity shop and select a load of different materials. There's one just down the road which has a thirty pence sale on all clothes every Thursday. I could go tomorrow after signing on. I could actually make something again. Is that because he's a writer? Is his creativity rubbing off on me too?

He isn't out there any more, but there is a note, and a present. It's some kind of cuddly toy, one of those ones with the huge plastic eyes that they sell in card shops. The handwriting is so illegible this time that I can't read what it says; but the words "Matilda", "Devoted", "Hate", "Lacy" and possibly "cunt" are all in there.

MOTHER

If I find myself listening to The National, before moving down *through* Damien Rice, *to* Joy Division, *then it's very likely I'm sinking into one of my moods. If I'm listening to* Joy Division's Isolation *over and over, then I'm already there.* She's Lost Control *is for the phase when I get angry about it all.*

I mostly listen to music on the long bus journey back from seeing my psychiatrist.

Right now I'm listening to it for a different reason. I'm trying to write a memoir and its helping me visualise my past. Each song links me to all the other times I have heard it in my life.

But it turns out I'm not quite ready to write about those times yet so I'm writing this instead. The tutor at my writing class says that keeping a journal while you're working on a project of any size is really helpful because you'll keep going back and looking over it and you can follow the path of your thinking. And because I'm writing a memoir maybe the two will merge together anyway. It's not for publication…well…I might self-publish, but it's just a thing to do so that I can say I've done it really.

Something I could maybe leave to my daughter.

TILDA

Twenty-one.

That's the number of days they've decided to keep me locked up. Because I fainted. It's not fair. Fuck them. Fuck them all. I'm not allowed to sit up, so I'm lying on my belly writing this. My IV is twisted but I hope the bastard falls out. It's their fault. They're the ones who shoved this notebook at me and told me to write. Write what?

I can't concentrate for long.

They wheeled in a TV today but my legs are weak after lying in bed for days so I can't get up and change the channel without asking them for the remote, and they'll only let me watch certain things. So no eighteens, or anything "triggering" leaving all the things I hate – daytime soaps, then game shows, then evening soaps.

One meeting and twenty-one days transform into six months. All these old retired lawyers gather round with your doctors and discuss you. They call it a "review" but seems more like a fucking trial to me. It almost makes me want to eat again. Sorry. Can't write much. Brain is squelching.

If I eat yogurt and cereal for breakfast and three fatty milkshake things a day I'm allowed to walk myself to the toilet and sit in the lounge with everyone else for an hour.

Some days I do it. But others…I have this thing in my head that stops me. When I first got in I thought this was all about the fainting. That if I ate enough to not collapse again, they'd let me go. It's more complicated than that. It's—

I poisoned a child. What if Mia… What if its mother wants to poison me back? Doesn't she have a right to? What if she knows one of the kitchen staff? Or a way to sneak into the factory where they process…or knows someone who drives the food van or…

Fed up of talking. Not going to fucking talk to you too.

Psychologists, psychiatrists, psychiatric nurses, psychotic patients, psy psy psy psy.

They repeat quiz show episodes several times in a day. They. Repeat. Them. They repeat them.

It's itchy hot in here. I fell asleep and someone stole the fan I'd stowed away. I've had my hour in the lounge so I can't get up and find it. They have the heating on even though it's a heatwave outside. I know it's definitely a heatwave because they left on one of the channels with sixty-second news updates in between every programme.

I've waited until the ones with staff following them have all gone to the toilet or to their rooms. Now there is only one woman watching us in the lounge and she's pretty big. I doubt she's going to be able to catch me.

I did it… well, kind of. I'm back here now.

I walked over to the pool table. Her eyes didn't even follow me. She was focused on a patch in the carpet, probably bored out of her mind. I picked up a cue and shot a ball into the far corner. The one near the Fire Exit. Then I wandered over there. Taking my time. A slow step back, made the bar for the fire door maybe thirty centimetres away, I was very aware that I needed to shove it and start running all in one movement in order to get a head start, she might be fat, but my legs have very little muscle on them, even now I've put a horrendous amount of weight on.

She didn't even look my way.

I shove and go before the alarm even has a chance to start ringing –. I'm three steps out and it's only just started. Then I'm running full pelt and I hear the lone woman shout for help. My legs are stiffer than I thought they would be, but I keep looking behind me and the distance between us keeps growing.

It seems to be working— Until more staff come pouring out, and they're catching up quickly. I know I need to reach the trees. I've planned this all out. I need to get to the trees and climb one. It came up in a film I was watching last night. The place people always forget to look is upward.

MOTHER

When I imagine things they play as clearly as a film on my laptop. But those periods where I felt nothing, when I was numb on the sofa for months, I can't remember any of it. All I know is what the men tell me.

Which they try not to do, until it all comes out the first time we have an argument. Then whoever I'm with screams it all in my face and leaves.

I'm never loveable enough for them to overlook the crazy forever.

Why do I want to write a memoir?

Someone looking in from the outside would see my life as something incredibly dull. What they don't realise is that I live entirely on the inside. It's all about the things going on in my head.

I tried to write a novel once, but all the characters ended up having my voice. It was just multiples of me talking.

MATILDA

23rd August 2015

Don't call me stupid. That's what my Mother would say about me. I'm waiting for him in a café. Yes. I've decided to give him a second chance.

He grinned as soon as he saw me, almost jumped over the doorway, then handed me a folded package of refill pad paper, with his handwriting scrawled all over them.

"Read it later" he hisses and then giggles. I've never seen him laugh before, but there he was. Giggling. I wasn't sure I liked it but I went along with him. I'm going to quickly write down what we said before I forget it all, so sorry if my writing is a bit messy.

"Want a coffee?"

"No."

He shook his head too and then did something funny with his hands.

"I'm already fizzy."

I laughed, but this time he didn't. His eyes went all wide and serious.

"Let's go somewhere."

"Where?"

"On holiday again. We need a—"

"We just got back—"

"So? I have money!"

"I'm trying to get a job."

"Seriously?"

"Not really. But I might be!"

"Come on! Let's go. We could travel the world."

"We're not in a fucking Rom-com"

"I'm serious."

"No."

"Why not?"

"You left me alone Thomas."

"I didn't."

"You did. You kept leaving me in the apartment."

"That's not true."

"Yeah. It is."

"Look. I love you Matty…"

"I don't like that."

"What? You don't feel this—"

"No. 'Matty'. That's not my name."

"Nonsense. It's 'Tilda' you don't like."

"I like 'Matilda'."

"I don't care what the fuck you're called. I love you."

I shake my head.

"What?" he shouted at me.

"We haven't… You know… We haven't even…"

Then he stood up, stared down at me. Started belting his words out in my face.

"I know you enough to know I love you don't you have

any idea how strange that is for me"

He spoke just like that, with no punctuation. People were staring at us.

"Sit down."

"What?" he looked at me suspiciously.

"Sit down."

"No fucking way."

There was a long pause, then for some reason I started laughing. Then he started laughing. The people in the café pretended to go back to their own conversations.

He still didn't sit down.

"Now let's go have sex!"

And that's how I got to this point. Scrawling this down, because I know it's all going to go wrong, and I want to learn something from it when I read it back through in the future. Maybe you'll learn something from it too, dear reader.

MOTHER

I'm aware I'm full of contradictions. I can't carry a thought from one day to the next. It's like I get reset every night I go to sleep. So the chances of this being a coherent story are pretty low.

That's why I invest so much in things. Nothing expensive. Notebooks, books, DVDs. Things I can externalise what goes on in my brain with.

So maybe I'm just writing this to fill notebooks.

I've been reading Carrie Fisher's books ever since she died. She writes about mental illness but she doesn't write self-help. She accepts that some illnesses last a lifetime, that defeats and victories are only temporary.

Yet I don't think I'll write my memoir like she writes hers. Although I like the finished product, she writes to fit the humour rather than writing the humour to fit the story.

TILDA

They didn't say much in front of me, but I can tell Doctor Peters is pissed off. The on-call gave me way too high a dosage for my weight. I still can't move. I never got to the tree. I have bruised wrists and ankles where they held me, like a crime show victim. I haven't eaten any of their gunky food or drank their fucking milkshakes since they got me.

During visiting hours I can switch off the music channels that are usually a constant in the lounge. It's the only time the place is quiet.

I'm curled up with my feet up on the sofa when my Key Nurse, Amy, approaches. Usually that means something is wrong.

"Hello Tilda. How are you feeling?"

I shrug. Anything more would get analysed.

"Do you feel up to a visitor?"

My lips edge together and I bite them hard. He's finally forgiven me. He's finally come to see me.

I grin. I nod.

"It can't be off the ward because of your recent absconsion, but they could come through here if you want?"

I nod again. Words don't quite seem right. Anyway, my face is tight holding up its inevitable smile.

Maybe he wants me back.

Amy brings in my mother.

She returns the smile I'm holding, but as soon as I register her fully my face drops.

"Hello," she says.

I can't even say hello to her. She sits down on the sofa next to me and I edge away.

"Tilda. Its me."

She thinks I'm so far gone I don't know who she is. If only I was. I would give anything to be convinced its David sat there.

"I can fucking see that."

MOTHER

I think I'm a very genuine person.

Even my daughter knows my secrets. I've always taught her she can tell me anything. And she does…eventually. Sometimes too late. When it's too late it seems like I couldn't have helped. But maybe to her it seems like I can never help, because when she has come to me early its only ever been with things I couldn't possibly help with. It's the things she comes to me with too late which I could have helped with.

At least I showed up. I didn't stay long. But I showed up.

MATILDA

4th September 2015

I'm not in the mood for "Hey" today.

I was sat in Thomas' living room. He was out meeting the editor for his new collection. He says it's about the feeling of eroticism in the tension before a hailstorm. Which is kind of beautiful but nonsensical, a lot like him. That's when the phone rang.

"Matilda?" a strange voice said down the phone.

"Yes"

"Sorry, we don't know your surname. Thomas Markus has you as his I.C.E. number."

"His what?" I ask.

"In Case of Emergency." I drop my knees down onto the sofa.

"Has there been an accident?"

"Are you a family member?"

"If there's been an accident he would want me to know what's happened."

"How well do you know Thomas?"

Not at all.

"Intimately."

"Are you aware of his disorder?"

Nope.

"Of course. Which hospital is he in?"

"He's being moved to Primrose Vale Psychiatric. Tonight. They'll let you see him tomorrow. I think their visiting is six till eight but maybe phone them and ask."

"Hello?"

"Matilda?"

I cough to cover up my silence.

"Yes. Primrose…"

"Primrose Vale."

"Right. Do they have a number or a website or something?"

"It's the same one he was in last time."

"Yes…of course…sorry, I'd forgotten the name."

"Ok Matilda. Can I trust you to phone his parents?"

"Yeah."

"Thank you. Bye."

I don't say anything. I just hang up.

I don't even know his parent's names. I don't even know if they're alive.

Just before I started writing I Googled "Primrose Vale Psychiatric". It's run privately. It's medium secure. I've been trying to imagine what he's done to need "medium security". Isn't that like how they class prisons?

Now I'm trying to stop imagining what he's done to need to be in "medium security".

Hello. Well… I went…

I sat in the waiting room for what felt like hours. It was

inside an airlock. I went to the desk and then they sent me through and locked the door behind me. Then there was another locked door which led to the visiting room. No bars or anything though. They both looked like ordinary automatic doors, only they could be locked.

"Primrose Vale" was emblazoned on a noticeboard with no notes on it just across from me. I still spent most of my time examining that. There wasn't much else to look at. The wall it was on was green, the wall at a right angle to that was purple. It was an awful colour mix.

Eventually a member of staff opened the second locked door, their keys jangling on an elastic thread the whole time.

"Matilda Martins?"

I stand up. She takes me through and then locks the door behind us.

She unlocks the door of a side room and signals that I should go inside there next. She comes in after me. It's barely bigger than a cupboard. She reaches down and holds up a metal detector.

"Can you stand like this for me?"

She splays her legs and arms wide, I copy.

She runs the metal detector over her watch to make sure it works; then runs it over my body.

"Could you lift your feet up?"

I lift my feet. Left, then right.

She smiles. I seem to have passed the test. Maybe the test was to see if I would lift them both up together.

She leads me back out of the room and locks the door behind us. Then she shows me down a corridor of other side rooms. These are the visiting rooms and most of them are full of chatting families.

When we reach an empty one she opens the door to let me in. Tells me to sit and wait while she goes to get him.

MOTHER

In the writing class the tutor gave me a list of mental health memoirs. I haven't heard of most of the people on the list, but a lot of them are 99p books on Amazon so I've ordered a few. Janet Frame, Jenny Diski, Elyn Saks, Barbara Taylor, a musician called James Rhodes… They're nearly all women.

Maybe the market is already too saturated?

Then again, ever since you could pay to go and see patients chained up in Bedlam people have been fascinated by watching the mentally ill. Seeing how mad mad could get.

At least when we write about it we're in control.

I think I'm falling in love with the tutor. She's maybe ten years younger than me, and everyone looks good at that distance, but I think this is something more than that. It's her wiry hair and Harry Potter style glasses which really get to me.

I couldn't get my thoughts to shift from my head to the paper, so I started watching TV with a pen in my hand.

There's something about having too much silence to concentrate in; it makes my brain constipated. Having something on in the background loosens everything up and ideas start coming spontaneously again.

I can see myself on my laptop screen. Pen in my lips like I'm smoking it. Hair in waves, forced outwards by over-ear headphones. A few flecks of grey hair. I should brush it more. My mother used to call it a nest and I'd imagine how much I'd like tiny chicks to hatch out of it.

TILDA

Misty Upman's death is all over the news. I hadn't heard of her before and I feel bad about that. Apparently she was in that film recently that was adapted from a play. The one with Meryl Streep and that lot in it. I think she must have killed herself, because one of the nurses came in pretty quick and switched the TV off. Said we weren't allowed to watch the news for a few days.

I haven't wanted to tell you because I can't quite believe it's true. I mean— I'm not sure whether or not I want it to be true. After all that fighting to make me stay here, they're suddenly saying my section is up in eight days. I'm average now: average weight, average, medicated brain. I suppose other people need the bed more. When I questioned it after the meeting they just gave me more Lorazepam. It's so strange. I don't think I want to go. I genuinely don't… this place feels so safe. It's horrible, but if I do something bad I know they're going to hold me down until I stop. Away from here, well, anything could happen and no-one would even care. I don't know…there's just something about this place…I don't know…I'm confused…it's just so fucking sudden. It's so fucking sudden. I'd started to trust this place. The staff…the rhythm…the meals…I can eat again when the meals are prescribed but on my own…

Thought about it. Now I'm a "safe" weight, if they think I'm going to eat when I get out they have another thing coming.

Key Nurse Amy says I can stay on voluntarily after the section ends. That even though they won't renew it doesn't mean I have to go. I asked her why the fuck I'd want to stay. I say I might as well walk out right now. She says she'd have to run after me because the section lasts six more days so I'm still under it. I ask what the fuck the point of that is and she tells me off for swearing.

I did it. I ran. And they restrained me again. I fought back hard so they stabbed me in the arse with Haloperidol. There is no way they can let me go now. I kicked one of the nurses square in the balls. He called me a "bugger".

Amy says last night was a just a blip. A fucking blip. They've prescribed me regular Lorazepam, but didn't specify how long for. Whether my… five days now…have been increased. But she didn't mention discharge either.

Fuck her.

MATILDA

11th September 2015

We're in the small room where they keep Thomas. It's not a cell. There are no bars, but there is a slatted observation window on the door. Two nurses sit beyond it, watching us over the top of cheap magazines.

Thomas sits and gasps the best breaths he can manage. There is something holding him back. I've watched enough asylum horror films to know it's probably the meds. I reach over and hold his hand, but it only makes him more nervous so I pull away again.

"Never thought…" he mutters.

"Jesus what do they have you on?" I think, but decide not to say.

"I didn't want you to…come…here"

"It's nothing to be ashamed of."

"But it is."

"I haven't called your parents. Can I have their numbers?"

"I can't remember." His slow speech makes it even easier to tell that he's lying.

"Do you have your phone? Or do they?"

"I don't know."

"Come on Thomas."

He shakes his head. He hasn't looked at me the entire time

– except that glare when I took his hand, and I'm not trying that again just to get a look.

"Thomas—" I say and then realise I have absolutely nothing else to say to follow it up. How can he have gone from screaming "Let's have sex!" in public to this in under a week. They shouldn't have let me see him like this. The staff should have told me he wasn't ready.

Then I look at him and know they couldn't have stopped me. I had to come. I would have demanded to see him.

"Thomas. I don't care about any of this. I mean…I do care about you…I don't…I don't mind that you're in here. I'm still with you…"

He laughs. It's cruel.

"Then why have you left me here alone? You and my fucking parents. What's the point of calling them when I've got you to act just like they would."

"I'm not going to just leave you. I'll visit you every day."

"They won't let you."

"Every day they let me then."

"Exactly what my parents would say, and that's where the compromises start—"

"What? Do you want me to break in?"

"If you fucking have to! Yes!"

He's stood up. I can see one of the nurses watching us, and getting itchy.

"Sit down Thomas." I try to coax him back down.

"I don't want to fucking sit down!"

I don't fight him any further. The truth is I want out of

that room. Not forever. Just today. I need to come up for air.

I think he was simply leaning forward, but evidently they thought he was going for me. The nurses barge in, just like I could have imagined. I back off and leave the room before they even start shouting for me to go. Outside I try to slap my palms against my forehead but hit my eyes instead. I don't listen. I refuse to listen. And then I leave.

TILDA

This isn't what is supposed to happen. I'm not safe. They have that doctor coming in to see me. I'm sat on the flat blue bed in the treatment room. I can't stand up for long without feeling dizzy. Yet my weight is stubbornly average. When I get on the scales now they say "Well done!" in such high pitched cheery voices that I want to punch them out.

It's not entirely my fault – although recently I have had a lapse in judgement – it's the pills; they make you so hungry and slow the metabolism down. They don't even work. I asked them all about it last week:

"How do they work though?"

"They balance out the chemicals in your brain."

"Which chemicals?"

"Serotonin, Dopamine mostly."

"How?"

"They stop the chemicals from being sucked out of your blood."

"So I have too little Serotonin and Dopamine."

"You could say that."

"You could say that?"

"No-one really knows for sure how they work. The brain is largely an unexplored thing. Maybe the last unexplored thing—"

I must have looked pretty startled because he shook his

head, trying to take back everything.

"The point is they work."

Dr Whatever is here. I'll write again later.

As soon as he walked in he got a needle out of the cupboard and I felt my veins crawling up and away from my skin. There's a nurse and she signals for me to pull my sleeve up. I don't. Dr Whatever hides the needle under a giant sheet of pale blue toilet paper.

"Why don't you roll your sleeve down now..." he genuinely coughs whilst trying to remember my name "...Matilda."

"It's Tilda."

"Tilda, hinny, roll up your sleeve," says the nurse.

I do it and they scrape away with the needle at one arm and then the other.

"Hinny, we're going to have to try your hand."

I sit on my hands.

"Ok then," mutters Dr Whatever. He is momentarily fazed.

"I need to check your stomach. Can you lie on the table, pull the t-shirt up?

I do as he says. I know he'll have cold hands, and he does. Like ice. He feels up close to my boobs and then moves down to the (now wide) expanse around my belly-button.

For the first time in a while I think about the kid. How he would have been joined to his mother in the womb.

When I look up again Dr Whatever has paused. He may have been like that for a while. He's making a weird noise.

"What?"

"Just a second," says Dr Whatever and moves his hand in a small circle, like I'm an Ouiji board.

"What?" I ask again.

"There's something there," he says.

"Yeah, my fucking stomach."

"Language," says the nurse, on autopilot.

"This needs checking out."

"Well she's being discharged soon," says the nurse.

"Oh. Ok, well I'll give you a note then… emm…Tilda. Then you can take it to your GP when you get out."

I nod as if I care.

MATILDA

25th September 2015

I'm rocking in the rocking chair, that's why my handwriting is like this, and it's like I'm somehow connected to Thomas. It's as if I know for sure that he is sat somewhere, probably on a hospital bed, maybe on a seat in their lounge, rocking away his thoughts too. Externally rocking is an almost silent action; but internally it's like a siren that disintegrates everything in your head. The good things are splintered, but also the bad. Give it a try next time you are upset.

But I need to stop rocking because I need to think. I've decided something. I've decided to get Thomas out of there. He needs to get better, but that hospital, it isn't the right place for him. All he gets in there are drugs. Yesterday I tried to visit him, but they said he was too worked up. They asked about his parents again and I said I still couldn't get hold of them. I don't feel guilty about it. They'd be happy he was in there. They aren't good for him either. I can fix him.

I've spoken to a solicitor. I told him Thomas was my husband and he said that a hearing could be demanded. He asked me how long Thomas' section lasted for, whether it was for assessment or treatment, and I had to admit I didn't know. He seemed a little suspicious after that, but I insisted I would go into the hospital and find out this afternoon. I have to be prepared this time and not seemed shocked by it all again. I need to convince them all that he could come home with me and I'd know what to do – I've been looking a lot of stuff up on the internet.

I'm in again and waiting for him in the visitors room. This time they seem less rushed, and even offer me a cup of coffee. I accept and am presented with a polystyrene cup full of lukewarm sludge. I thank the nurse anyway. She lets me know that Thomas is taking his mid-afternoon meds and so he might be a few minutes. Half an hour later I hear the buzz of the airlock door to the ward. Two nurses walk either side of Thomas, I stand up as they enter.

"We'll be right outside." Says the bulkiest of the pair. The other helps Thomas fall awkwardly into his seat and then leaves too.

"Hey Thomas."

It's like his eyes have drifted and got stuck in a diagonally downward angle.

"Thomas. I'm going to get you out."

"Is this because of Copenhagen?"

I'm so surprised by him speaking that I fail to take in what he's said.

"What?"

He mimics my voice.

"You left me. You left me in the villa Thomas. You left me."

He thinks that is the same as this?

"I'm sorry. I had to do some thinking."

Silence returns. The eyes head back downwards.

"I was reading about Yves Saint Laurent and how his friends helped him so he could live outside the hospital—"

"Fuck off Matty. You don't want me."

I don't correct him on the name.

"I fucking do," I say.

"Why?"

"What?"

"Why do you want me?"

"Because… I do."

"Crazy may be many things, buts it's interesting. Isn't it?"

"I don't understand."

"You were bored without me. And now I'm in here and you're bored again. Not even your fucking books can touch it, it has to be me. You have to drag me out of here," he says.

"That's not— I wasn't bored…I'm not bored…"

"Really? What did you have in your life before me?"

"Thomas—"

"Tell me. Matilda. What did you have?"

"I love you."

"Fuck off."

"You need to get out of here Thomas. This place is bad for you," I say.

"Fuck off. You don't know what I need," he says.

Are you ok with swearing? Should I start bleeping it out?

"In case you haven't noticed you don't have anyone else.

I don't know if you ever had any friends but they evidently don't care now. And your parents, where are they exactly?"

"Have you even bothered to phone them? Or do you want the nutter to yourself?"

"I'm your only way out of here."

"I don't want out," he says.

TILDA

Three days until the end of the section, and after all Key Nurse Amy's protestations they've only just let me know they have a place for me. That's what they said:

"We've found a place for you Matilda."

"It's Tilda."

"Tilda."

I nod.

"It's called supported accommodation. Do you know what that means?"

"Like for old people?"

My nan died in supported housing.

"It's somewhere you choose to live. It's not a section. It's a house you share with other people, but where you'll also have twenty-four hour support from staff."

"Doesn't sound all that much different from here."

"It will be very different."

"How?"

"It'll be better. Great access to therapy for one thing. You'll do group psychotherapy twice a week. And the staff will have more time for you there. It's a longer term solution."

I didn't know I was a problem in need of a solution; I don't say anything but I pull a face. The nurse gets stroppy.

"Look, Tilda, it's your choice whether you go or not, but a lot of people here would really love this opportunity and it's going to cost a lot of public money to get you there. So think carefully about it."

I wake up and feel like I haven't got a face. Not that it's been cut off or anything, just that I don't have one. It's week two here, not that I need to count the days and weeks any more. No section. Life here lacks the rhythm of the hospital. At least there I got woken up and put to sleep with sleeping pills. Here there is a replacement service of overwhelming lethargy. I'm with three other women. We each have our own bedroom but scuttle around avoiding each other in the rest of the house. No-one here has a job so there is a lot of Jeremy Kyle. Kyle was always banned in the hospital. There is a comforting pattern to the shows, build up, lies, lie detector results, explosion of emotions— next arguing family.

Group therapy gives Tuesday and Thursday some kind of shape. It lasts two hours on each afternoon. On the days in between, when there is no session I'm always either dreading it or recovering from it. There are some other less-precise groups covering the rest of the weekdays, but I suspect they're more to entertain the staff than us. I kind of like Art Therapy, but it's all glitter pens and no oil paints.

MATILDA

5th October 2015

Hey,

people who have been away are supposed to relish sleeping in their own beds again. Thomas has been up there for two days now. I suppose it's not actually his own bed, it's one of my beds, but it's still not in an institution. I gave him the spare room. He accepts his pills but no food. I'm sat downstairs watching a documentary on Anais Nin and writing this. Low volume so I can hear if he moves. I've just ordered a volume of Nin's diaries and a couple of other things from Amazon.

Do you think Amazon is soulless? There's something about that yellow smile…

I've watched to the end of the documentary and he still hasn't moved. His stuff is in the hall. I creep up to it, like he was inside one of the rucksacks, and pull a bag back to the sitting room like prey. Stinking clothes spill out, which is good because I can say I smelt them inside and opened the bag to put them in the wash.

Amongst the clothes there is an open envelope. I slide it wide with my finger and read. It is a letter from Thomas' psychiatrist to his GP. At the top it lists his diagnoses. I read them as a poem of explanations.

AXIS I: Bipolar Disorder
Borderline Personality Disorder
Post Traumatic Stress Disorder.

AXIS II: Possible Aspergers

Also some symptoms of dissociation found.

I fold it up and return it to the envelope.

I want him to come down and see me, so I turn the TV right up and put a horror film on. It's a terrible one with over-dramatic music. He can't possibly sleep through it.

Was it a mistake? Bringing him home? Would I have done this for anyone else? Would I have done this two months ago, before I met him? Who am I any more?

TILDA

I've been writing. Poems mostly. The writing group here got me started. When I was at school I wanted to be a playwright, mostly because I liked the way the word sounds. Poems are easier somehow. They're about intense emotions, which I have, and channelling them, which I need more practise in. Everything still seems so pointless to me, yet I'm closer to feeling happy when I'm writing than at any other time. The staff keep asking what I write or if they can read a little bit; but they'll just analyse it like everything else I do here and I want something for myself.

MATILDA

21st October 2015

Dear, dear reader. There has been progress. Thomas is sitting down here with me – vegetating in front of a game show, but it's still something. He seems to be barely concentrating, like he's completely spaced, but then when I try to put a film on he grunts at me. He reminds me of a cat I once had who would snooze and then suddenly leap up and growl if a car went past.

He never sits back any more. He's always on the edge of his seat, staring at the flashing lights and glib faces. He also smokes. I'm not sure if he did before, but he's making no effort to hide it now. The landlord came for the rent the other day and I think he smelt it. He hasn't made a comment yet though.

I don't know if I can go out or not. I ask him if he wants to go to the shops and he ignores me. We're going to run out of milk. There is still no word from his parents, even though the hospital finally got through to them.

I've locked up the knives and decided I'm going out. He is asleep so he probably won't even notice. I need some fucking milk to make a fucking cup of tea.

Today his social worker showed up at the house and said she'd booked an appointment with him yesterday, but he didn't show. He didn't even tell me, but it made me look bad for not getting him there so I didn't have enough time to wake him. It was made worse because I had to let her in then and there and Thomas was still sleeping in at two in the afternoon.

I run upstairs, asking her to wait in the hall whilst I try and get him dressed and looking like he hasn't just woken up.

I open the curtains and pull the cover off him, whisper "Up. Now." But all he does is mumble that his mouth is dry. I carefully feed him some water and then snatch it away again.

"Up."

He claws around like a mole. I throw some clothes at him and run back down to the social worker, but she's already seen the kitchen. Fuck.

"You two eating alright?"

"Yeah. Fine. Lots of vegetables."

She eyes the tins of beans I've been serving him for most meals.

"I don't get a chance to go to the shops much."

"Eating healthily is key to Thomas' recovery."

"MmmmHmmm."

Hurry up Thomas. Hurry up.

"And you have to make sure you make time for yourself to go out. You have to keep living your life."

How the hell am I supposed to do that? I nod in agreement.

That's when Thomas comes down the stairs, yawning and wearing an inside out top.

"Thomas!" I shout and point at him like an idiot.

The social worker takes a good look at him.

"Hello Thomas."

Thomas nods and then slumps onto the sofa. I grab the remote so that he doesn't switch the game shows on.

"Thomas. Why didn't you tell Matilda I was coming?"

Thomas shrugs.

The social worker takes this in as if she has some kind of deep understanding of him.

"Matilda. Maybe it would be best if you left us alone to chat."

I want to argue but I don't. I just get out of there. I'm perched on the bed upstairs. The bitch closed the door. I can't hear what they're saying, so I'm writing this instead.

TILDA

I don't feel right. I'm hot. My stomach has this vague ache , and I can't stop chewing my lip. I told the staff but they just said it was anxiety. Tell them you sneezed and they'll say its anxiety.

Everyone's just as into celeb magazines here as they were in the hospital. This place is dull and writing only helps temporarily. My brain keeps stuttering back to thoughts of self-harm because it has nothing else to do. It's echoing round my head. All the blood. Black blood is best. It kind of slides out.

When I need distracting but I don't have the energy to write pop songs help and horror films help. I haven't found much else. I listen to both at the highest volume my headphones can handle. Which is pretty loud even with noise cancelling monsters. I have to sit upstairs with them or everyone stares at me.

Today I can't stop being sick. One of the other clients – Anne – keeps bitching about it. She thinks I'm bulemic and keeps saying that I don't have to rub it in her face (whilst she eats her second packet of biscuits of the day). I can't stop it, even though the staff will be suspicious soon enough.

Up half the night and all I wrote is "My brain is like a sci-fi film. It keeps skipping over itself across time and space. But my bellyache is constant and I think it's getting worse."

When the staff got up I told them about the pain again. They said they would take me over to the doctors if I really wanted them to. I don't think I'll go. They said I'd have to take responsibility and phone up myself for the appointment. I hate using the phone. You can't tell what the person on the other end really thinks of you and then I obsess about it for hours after. Plus voices that come from nowhere really freak me out.

I don't think I desperately need to go anyway.

It's probably just a UTI. It'll go away.

I'll buy some cranberry juice tomorrow. It'll be fine.

MATILDA

I don't know who to address this to any more. No-one's going to read it. Are they? Are you?

I can't leave the house so I've been reading more than ever; then ordering more and more books online. The postman arriving with parcels has become the highlight of my day, even though Thomas makes a lot of fuss every time the door rings. I think it reminds him of the alarm bell in the hospital. I try to listen out for the sound of the postman on the gravel so I can get to the door before he presses the bell.

At least Thomas gets out of bed now, though only to sit plumbed into the telly – but that's ok. I ordered a portable DVD player so I can space out the books with some films and leave him with the TV. Today its *Gentlemen Prefer Blondes*. I haven't watched it for so long, long enough that I'm slightly unfamiliar with it and can enjoy it again.

Or not recite the words anyway.

It's a strange fantasy of a film, I wish men were that enthusiastic about anything in real life. Women having such silly voices could also be entertaining. I want to bounce on beds and speak like a child. It's a weird wish but it looks so good.

I can't get caught up in it as usual though. I always have to have at least one eye on Thomas

Me and Thomas we…

We're sat on the sofa together and I'm not used to him getting in this close. I think he's thinking about moving his hand to my knee. Its wavering a bit anyway. I pull the headphones out of my ears but leave the DVD playing.

"Thomas?"

He's pulling at my jeans. Clumsily trying to yank them down. I lean in and kiss him instead. Then I move his hands to my top and let him pull it off over my head. I pull away the bra hooks myself because his hands are shaking. Then I grab his T-shirt away. He's put on weight since the last time I saw him, but I don't care. He's warm, and pushes his body against me. I realise that skin touching skin is such an odd sensation. Smoothness but with occasional sweaty patches that make our movements catch a little. He rams upwards and misses a couple of times, so I reach down and steer him in.

Do you like watching us have sex?

He jerks around a bit, gets me going a little, but finishes quickly. I mutter that it's ok and let him fall off me. He is sound asleep by the time I notice this is an uncomfortable position to lie in so I have to gently lift his hand and foot so that I can turn over. The sofa is barely big enough for both of us, but I lie there and enjoy the contact.

It's been a couple of hours now and I've pulled the headphones out of the DVD player and started the film again. I'm playing it quietly so that I can still listen to his breathing alongside the dialogue. I've got this notebook balanced on the arm of the chair. In an hour or so I'll order in something for dinner. I'm deeply hungry in a way only greasy food will help.

TILDA

"It's really triggering for me—"

"I can't help it!"

"Tilda, let Jenny speak."

"I'm not making myself sick!"

"We all know you are and you need to admit it," says Chloe, Jenny's bitchy mate. Then she puts her hand on Jenny's shoulder. "Jenny has serious problems with food and you know that."

I wait for the psychotherapist to intervene, to maybe defend me, but she seems to be practising what she calls "The Art of Listening".

"I'm not doing it on purpose, I think I'm ill," I insist.

"It's natural for you to rationalise your actions Tilda." Now the therapist speaks.

"I'm not making it up."

"Then why haven't you gone to the Doctors?" barks Jenny.

I get up and leave. All the therapist woman says when I slam the door is: "Come back when you can."

I storm upstairs and blast my music so that they can definitely hear it in the session below.

I am never doing psychotherapy again.

Running up the stairs has made my stomach hurt, so I throw up into the sink.

Someone is knocking on the door. I can tell it's Richard, one of the support workers, because he does a silly knock.

"I'm busy," I shout at him, but I turn the music down a bit.

"I've made an appointment with the GP tomorrow," he calls though the door. "I'll take you down if you like."

I open the door. I like trips out with Richard. He knows this café owner who makes him special cakes. Even after just puking I want one of those cakes.

"Ok," I say to him.

"And you know you're supposed to go back in again before the end if you leave group. They're not very happy with you."

"I know."

"It's hard. It's going to keep being hard. But it's good for you." He smiles like he genuinely believes what he's saying. "Do you want to come down and play a board game?"

"No. I'm ok up here."

"Ok then," he says. I watch after him as he leaves and then close the door when he reaches the bottom of the stairs.

MATILDA

3rd November 2015

I'm going to have to make this quick. Yesterday I got a job. I've been applying ever since Thomas cooked me a meal after the third time we had sex. It was a romantic gesture, but in my head it was much more simple than that: a borderline. He can look after himself a bit more now. And we need the money. We really need the money. So I got a job.

It's a bit different to before – it's in a department store. I've always been a waitress, but I applied widely this time and now I'm a "Fashion Supervisor". It's basically a shop assistant post but I like the title anyway. I feel like I'm on *Mad Men* when Christina Hendricks briefly works outside the office. I start next Monday but the uniform is coming in the post tomorrow. I haven't told Thomas anything yet, I'm considering just leaving for work and seeing if he notices I'm gone. He only really pays attention to me for twenty minutes every evening. He's been feeding himself at lunch time for weeks now, baked beans and sausages at one o'clock without fail.

Am I doing the right thing?

Nope. Actually, don't answer that. I can decide for myself.

5th November 2015

The postman came to the door with the parcel and Thomas decided to answer it. How did he know? That one delivery. He usually get nervous about the postman, but not this one time. I ran downstairs but he already had the box open.

The argument is over now. He screamed at me for twenty minutes before giving me a chance to say anything. Then I put on a calm voice, which generally just sounds ridiculous, and explained it was only three days a week and that I'd be home to cook his main meal and do his meds. He isn't happy. He seems to think I'm abandoning him somehow.

I'm taking the job.

I've already taken the job.

Fuck this. I'm going to go watch *Girls*.

TILDA

Richard is holding my hand. We're at the GP's. Sitting here reminds me of when they took me out for my medical during the first week I was in hospital and I tried to run away. They grabbed me and sat me down and linked arms with me from either side. Everyone moved away from us, everyone looked away from us.

I still have that urge to run. I let Richard hold my hand, even though I want to shrink away from him and gradually curl up into a tighter and tighter ball until all that is left is this stupid, burning pain inside of me.

"It's ok." Richard has noticed something is wrong. I must be breathing funny. I can't speak so I nod.

"Seriously. She's just going to take a look at you."

I try to say "I want to go", but I can't. Richard hums a little in my ear, but then the nurse comes out and shouts my name.

"Want me to come in with you?" asks Richard. For some reason I shake my head, then I get up and leave with the nurse. Her uniform makes the backs of my legs itchy. She has black DMs on too though, so that's a small comfort.

I edge into the office around the door she's left half open. She's staring at the computer, clicking through notes.

"Hello," I suggest.

"Two seconds."

I sit in a chair to one side of her desk. Finally she looks up at me.

"What brings you here today?" It's there already, the sideways look and the patronising voice, she knows I'm mentally ill. Then she looks straight back at the computer. At least I don't have to struggle with the eye contact dilemma.

"I have this pain."

"Ok. Are you taking your medications?"

"Yes. What does that have to do with—"

"I just thought I should check before we start talking."

I can't think of anything to say.

"What are you here for?"

"My stomach hurts."

"Like a stomach ache?"

"No. It really hurts."

"How long for?"

"Since I left hospital. Two months ago. I saw a doctor there but…"

"Are you eating properly? Do you ever make yourself sick?"

"No!"

"But you have been diagnosed with an eating disorder."

"That was a while ago."

"You know, bulimia does have risks. That's what it's called when you make yourself sick."

"I know that… I'm not making myself sick again."

"That's ok."

She types something.

"Don't you even want to check my stomach?"

"Would that make you feel more comfortable?"

"Don't you need to?"

"Sure."

She waves her hand in the direction of the bed.

"No. It's ok."

I leave the room. I wait a little outside the door but she doesn't follow or shout.

I wander back through to the waiting room, then remember Richard is there, and start walking with the air of someone who knows what's going on.

"What did she say?"

"Yeah it's all fine."

MATILDA

10th November 2015

Sometimes it feels good to be back at work. And sometimes it feels like shit. I end up counting down to the end of my shift. Like earlier today: I'm stood at the counter, there's a stool but I'm not supposed to use it when customers are around – I have to look ready or something. In front of me a woman is breathing heavily and rustling through bags. There is a queue building but I can't interrupt her. Instead I glare at the teenager, the only member of staff below me, to go and get a proper adult to sort this out. But he doesn't get the meaning of the stare, or maybe he just ignores me.

After a few moments deliberating my best next move, I cough. She doesn't even look up. Now the woman behind her is sighing loudly. Together with the heavy breathing it becomes an oddly sexual rhythm: breathe, sigh, breathe, sigh. Rustle. I cough again, louder.

"Can I help you?"

"I have something I need to bring back," she mutters, and then immediately goes back to the rustling bags.

"Do you mind if I serve the customer behind you while you look?"

"Yes. Jesus. This place is supposed to have good service."

All I can think is "If I walk away will I get fired?". Two hours to go until the end of the day.

Thirty minutes.

And I'm thinking-does everyone else count down until the end of work? I'm not sure why I'm even doing this. I'm not sure I can see the point any more. I thought this job would be some kind of freedom, but it's just another kind of prison. I'm just arriving at eight thirty and counting down until six, three times a week. Then it's back to Thomas and all his (special has connotations in the disability world that aren't suitable here- so can we just go with "demands"?) demands. I'm always waiting for something more.

Ten minutes.

It's like water torture. How does everyone do this, every day? How do you get through the work day? No wonder Thomas is the way he is, he gets to escape all this…

Shut up brain. He's ill. His illness is nasty. How long would you survive on a psych ward?

Five minutes.

I'm leaving five minutes early. Fuck the system.

My boss saw me on the way out. I told him I was going to the toilet and I swear he winked at me.

He didn't wink at me. Did he?

I'm home. Thomas is somewhere on the sofa. I can't tell quite where because he's buried himself in smelly blankets. I could look for him and feed him… Or I could sit here, drink a cup of tea and watch *New Girl* for a bit first.

TILDA

I remember hating poetry in High School. Probably because they never actually got us to write any. Charlie, the woman who runs the Creative Writing group here, has lent me some books – Robert Lowell, Anne Sexton, Allen Ginsberg and one called *Asylum Girls*. Apparently they all write about mental illness, like I do. She gave me a book about Anne Sexton too: a transcript of her psychotherapy tapes. Not sure I actually want to read someone else's therapy when I have to sit through my own for four hours a week, but it was nice of her to lend them to me the books and she looked weirdly hopeful when she talked to me. Like she wanted to solve me. I suppose they all want to solve me in a way. It was less effort in hospital where most of the staff didn't give a fuck. I told Charlie I'd try to read them but it depends how I am.

The GP surgery phoned up yesterday and asked to speak to me. When the support worker who handed me the phone left to give me some privacy, I hung up the phone. Yes it still hurts but I think I'd better ignore it. I don't expect it will go away but I might forget it- it's always possible I might be imagining it.

MATILDA

20th November

Hey there,

Yes. I'm back to "Hey there". I'm trying to get you back on side.

I wish I got rejection letters like you see on films. Rejection emails are disgusting, nasty things. All they have to do is cut and paste and click a send button. Some of them seem genuine and have a couple of friendly things to say, but most of them spell my surname wrong, even though it's in my email address. I've been sending designs and photos of dresses I've made to indie shops. They all say no, or that I should do a few more in a different style and then get back to them, which is just a delayed no. I have always hated the word "maybe". Now I despise it even more. I'm running out of places to send things to, and because I've been finding their addresses online, youtube keeps suggesting fashion courses to me. I think I might go back to college. I can't tell my parents though, my dad would piss himself laughing if I said I was going to study fashion (it was bad enough when I wanted to study art), so I'm going to have to get a loan of some kind. I'd have to study part time so I could still help out Thomas and work at the store so that should bring the price down a bit. It's something I need to do. You agree right?

TILDA

Bleeps. Coughing. Several different coughs all going off with the discord of a child learning to play the violin. I have a curtain, but there is an obvious rule which hangs in the air – only the nurses are allowed to pull the curtains shut.

There is something inside me. The GP surgery finally caught Richard on the phone and ordered him to bring me back, something to do with the urine sample I gave them. They laid me down and prodded the bottom of my stomach. There is something growing in there. I was sent to A&E. Richard came too, he's waiting just outside right now, having a smoke or getting some coffee. I'm not allowed to eat or drink anything, but I couldn't anyway. They pressed so hard on my stomach so many times that I feel like something is rammed up against my spine and can't be dislodged. They keep asking me how long I've had the pain. I keep shaking my head.

I hope Richard brings me back something to read, I've been tracing the words on the back of a squirty pack of anti-bacterial soap over and over. I'm almost at the point where I'm so bored and nervous that I know the names of the chemicals off by heart. Sodium Lauryl Sulfate. Lauryl sounds like the name of a character in a George RR Martin novel. I wonder if she is friends with Triclosan. They could be lovers. Probably direct blood relations if we stick with the RR Martin theme. They lose their virginity to each other in a deep, wet cave. The muck from the surface of the rocks rubs off on Lauryl's back as Triclosan enters her. Or maybe she is on top for once…

Richard is back with a doctor on one side of him and a nurse on the other, like he's been escorted by police. They come over to me and pull the blanket away from my bare, unshaved legs.

"What?" I ask Richard.

Richard won't look at me.

Anne is not happy that I have cancer. She is no longer the most ill person in the house. I get my new meds handed out to me in case I forget, while she has to handle her own. She keeps threatening an overdose in group, staring at me each time. Still, the therapist doesn't mind if I don't say anything all session now, so I can just tune it all out and think up poems. I rush out to write them all down when group is over. I've been writing a lot of poems since I found out.

MATILDA

22nd November 2015

Hey future person(s),

So, I've been surfing around and I think I've found the answer. Evening classes. It's that or distance learning and I'd never have the motivation to teach myself. It also means I can keep the job. And don't you go worrying about Thomas, everything is better than ever with him.

Sort of.

Most of the time.

It's only one evening a week. I'll encourage him to invite friends round or something. He must have friends from before he was ill.

Anyway, he took the job hard at first, but that was fine in the end.

For now anyway.

Sort of.

I've booked myself on it. It's expensive but I've been saving small amounts up for myself for a while now, and I can pay in instalments.

I'll cook him something before I go.

This is going to be ok. Isn't it?

Eventually I'll be earning more money and that will be better for both of us.

I got the reading list today, I didn't realise Fashion was going to have textbooks, but it does and they cost a bomb. On top of the course costs. I ordered them all anyway. Even the cost can't stop me feeling kind of excited, I want to fill myself up with their big glossy pages then splurge it all out again to make something creative. I've been looking at sewing machines already even though the syllabus says it will be weeks before we're done with hand sewing.

The pictures in the books are ridiculous, but beautiful. Delicate things that could be destroyed so easily, even by just running for a bus…or like…climbing some stairs… I would never wear something like that but the buzz from thinking about making it—

At lot of the attraction is the materials. I love the texture of the different fabrics, how they feel when they come together. I should have ignored what my parents and the school were saying and done this course when I was eighteen.

TILDA

It's happening again. They're chucking me out. Richard finally told me, I think he's been holding it in for at least a week. I won't be talking to Richard again, no matter how many times he knocks on my door with his ridiculous knock.

He told me it's just because they're not equipped, that it's not something I've done.

I don't believe him. They want rid of me and they've been waiting for something like this to happen just for an excuse.

It is my fault. There is finally something physical that proves I am ill, it's not just how I feel any more, there is something bad growing inside me and I've always known it was there.

I wish I could talk this through with someone, but with Richard gone…

Who will drive me to appointments at the hospital?

They keep saying they're not equipped to deal with it. Am I supposed to be equipped?

I don't want to be ill. I've never really thought about it like that, whether I want to be ill or not doesn't make a difference, but now I have a horrible tear in my gut which is screaming that I don't want to be like this any more.

I want…

I wish… I want…

I want to stop now.

I have chemotherapy tomorrow. I move out next week. They found me an emergency flat from the week after. Everything is just a countdown to the next thing. Right now nothing can shift me from my bed.

MATILDA

30th November 2015

The teacher, John, is a towering man who punctuates classes every twenty minutes to go outside and smoke. He isn't thin, or muscled, or fat. He has this weird presence which isn't quite anything. For a fashion teacher he wears a lot of baggy grey items, but it somehow makes sense when you take the rest of him in. He tops it all off with a long black trenchcoat (which looks like it might be genuine World War Two). His fingers are yellow from all of the smoking; he does roll-ups not ready-made cigarettes, which I find impressive. I tried to roll one once and spilt someone else's tobacco all over the floor. I haven't tried again since. He's what mother would call an "odd creature" (one of the reasons she hasn't met Thomas yet).

Yesterday John did kind of tell me off for listening to Adele too loudly though, which was more than embarrassing. Her voice is one of the few modern singers I find deep enough to lose myself inside. I was just listening and sewing when John came up to me, picked up my ipod and scrawled through my albums, Edith Piaf, Billie Holliday, Bessie Smith and the rest. In the end he just turned the volume down. No-one else really listens to music so I'm not sure if its allowed, but the endless sound of the machines drives me mad.

Thomas hates Adele too. Some days I think Thomas hates everything. This morning he greeted me by shouting "Switch the fucking alarm off." He was up until two the night before; I know that because he kept me up too. He kept saying he felt like his skin wasn't real and that someone had tattooed words onto it without his permission. I rubbed some cream on in case it really was sore and then we eventually fell asleep, spooning on the bed. I was the big spoon and it quickly got uncomfortable, but eventually exhaustion grabbed me and I drifted into some kind of sleep.

"Tilda."

Shit. I get dragged back to earth by John, towering over and glowering down at me.

"Who knew one woman's howl could be so enthralling."

I pull my headphones out.

"Sorry."

"I was just saying I like your design— unlike your taste in music."

"Thank you."

"Well… are you going to tell us about it?" I realise the whole the class is watching, expecting me to speak.

I nod. I nod again, trying to think.

"Well, what was your starting point?"

"I like the colour. Turquoise. Then gold kind of fitted it all together—"

"What about the theme?"

"Hmmm?"

"The theme of the piece. What is it about?"

"It's about…colour…"

"And this pattern?"

"Yeah, its lush isn't it."

"Where did it come from?"

"I just started drawing and then used the printing silk screen to—"

"I'm trying to help you here Matilda. Can you tell me anything about how you felt when you were creating this piece?"

This question is easier.

"I was sad."

"You were sad?"

"Yes."

For some reason that didn't seem to be the right answer either.

TILDA

Richard tells me that I have to pack RIGHT NOW. I tell him I already have. I've bunged the books on Anne Sexton "borrowed" from the therapy lady and some about Eva Hesse and Louise Bourgeois from a library I will never return to. I packed a cardigan, a pair of jeans and a T-shirt too. I can re-stock from Primark once I get to wherever they dump me, and I really don't care what they do with the rest of my stuff.

I'm on the bus with my bag and an address. They said they would take me, but instead I woke up early and sneaked out before any of the staff surfaced. I want to get as far away as possible from them, as quickly as possible. The address is for a flat. I have nowhere else to go but I consider carrying on on the bus until the end of the line because I know services will have this new address too. I just want to escape all of them. I don't want to talk about my problems any more. Richard told me a CPN would be coming to see me twice a week as if it was a good thing.

I could go somewhere completely new and live in the nearest youth hostel. I have some money, I could do it. All I need is a room. Some books. And some art materials.

For the first time in a while I think about the kid and the pill packet. I deserve to die alone.

I need help.

I get off the bus at the right stop. A few streets away from where I think my new flat is, it takes me ten minutes of squinting at the map on the wall before I leave the bus stop. I should have let them take me over.

I walk along, slowly, in what I think is vaguely the right direction. Eventually, after only two wrong turns I get there. I light up outside and stare up at the tiny flat whose address is written on the sheet.

I don't have a key.

I look under the mat just in case, and there's one there so I shove it into the lock.

I step inside and the first thing I notice is the temperature drop. It's so much colder inside than out. I dig into my rucksack for that second cardigan. The building is empty and whitewashed like a mental hospital in an American film, complete with peeling gaps in the paint making ominous shapes. I touch the shapes. The walls are like ice and the texture in the wallpaper is like rusted metal. I have an urge to lick it, to taste if it is metallic as it seems.

MATILDA

I didn't want to.

No. That sounds like he forced me. He didn't.

It must have been in the back of my mind because I had no work left to do for the term project yet I still went in and sat in that room and sewed left over scraps into some kind of skirt until he struts in, a scarf bellowing out loud behind him. Not a winter scarf, a thin fabric one. One that might have been in fashion for men around the same time as bob length hair came back in.

I suppose it was because there was no-one else in the room.

That's not really an excuse though. Is it?

It was odd. Our teeth bashed together when we kissed. I think that's what jarred me to start feeling guilty. I didn't want to betray Thomas. I really didn't.

Anyway, after the clash and the guilt and us both rearranging our clothes, I didn't know what to say to him. So I asked him how much it was to buy a portfolio file for my work. He goes straight to the cupboard and gives me one for free. Then I kind of vaguely nod at him and leave.

If you can't speak to each other afterwards it probably wasn't the right thing to do.

PART TWO

MOTHER

I can't remember much of the first two years. Just exhaustion and screaming. Maybe I was so depressed I couldn't form memories. Maybe I just didn't have the time to form memories. I can recall this energy that sometimes came from nowhere and flooded me; only to recede just as quickly.

At the end of the two years, this ginger haired little girl tottered into my life. I genuinely can't remember her before she could walk. She was a very clumsy child. My boyfriend described her as a "tiny drunk person".

I can remember the rest of her, from then on. How she grew away from her small body, into something that would have towered over it. Her hair long down her back. At seventeen she cut it short. She should have told me she was going to do it. I would have collected all of it into a box and kept it safe.

I fell in love with her when she was three. I'd been fond of her beforehand, but it was only when that ginger mane of hair grew long and she became fierce that I began to love her as my daughter. We bonded painting together. Chaos Painting we called it. The walls, the floors, us, would all get splashed with paints, and we didn't care. I always wanted to study Fine Art.

I was angry when she didn't get the grades to go to university. She could have done if she'd tried. Maybe she'll get there eventually. Last time we spoke she was doing some kind of college course. Not exactly a degree, but better than nothing. If she does get into university I'll probably find out, but only because she'll come back here and be begging me for money.

When she was a little kid and she wanted money for something she could be so cute. She once picked up this teddy, and it was very ugly, it was some kind of monkey with pink hair, but she was really attracted to it for some reason. Anyway, she came up to me and said "Can we take him home?"

"Can we take him home?" What mother could say no to that? And anyway, it was pretty cheap.

I'm doped up today. Removed from the whole situation. Not on anything hard. I got prescribed these anti-histamines. They have "tiredness" as a side-effect, which is a code word for sedation. Anyway, I took twelve. Now I'm floating. I went to the shops this morning, it was really busy and I didn't feel anxious at all.

I hope you can buy these over the counter. You can get cough syrup that way, can't you? So why not?

Its Tilda when she does something wrong, Matilda the rest of the time.

Matilda is pretty. It's what I always wanted to call her. Her dad, for the brief moments he was even there, never liked it, so he called her Tilda. I think he just wanted to oppose me on everything. It was like there were two screaming babies in the house. But then again, even when he left, I'm pretty sure the house didn't get any quieter. I'm not sure why he left. That period melts in the same way I can't really remember Matilda before her third birthday.

I hate it when people make that face. Like they know you're lying. Only I'm not lying.

I just don't know what to say any more when people ask me if I have a child.

I'm not sure if I count as a mother any more.

I do want to…

I can't…

No child should be a reflection of me. I only make everything worse.

I hate Christmas. I'm not keen on anything built around worshipping two men (Jesus and Santa).

I hate writing that I hate things. I don't think I'm a hateful person; but sometimes things just stand out and there is nothing else I can say about them.

When I'm pissed off I listen to Devlin and Eminem. I suppose they're both out of date now, but I keep returning to them. I'm not sure I like them, it's just that hearing something that matches what is going on inside my head helps. I think it's venting really. Sometimes it just makes sense to put headphones on, turn the volume up on someone shouting violent things at you, and press the plastic of the headphones to your head.

I could just show up at her house, but I'm not that kind of mother. If she wants her privacy, she can have it.

I drove past her house this evening. All the lights were off. I sat and watched just for a few moments. I saw this bloke go up to her door and ring the doorbell, but he got no answer. That's Matilda for you.

I'm thinking about buying a cat. Probably a rescue cat, but you do still have to pay for those.

I suppose it's a sign that I'm lonely. It's a cliché really. But I just want to have contact with something living and warm.

I want a cat that will sit on my knee, that I could carry around.

In Japan they make special cat backpacks with windows in them, I've seen them on facebook.

I looked up my daughter on the internet. Her social media. She has all of them, but most of her posters are on the one just for pictures.

Her and some paintings.

Her and a dress someone has evidently home-made. Maybe she made it, that's what the post seems to be suggesting, but she never did have any fashion sense. She dressed as a boy when she was a kid and then when she was a teenager it was all hoodies no matter what I said.

Eventually I gave up trying to teach her how to do her hair. From the pictures online it looks like she never learnt. It's still in a shaggy mess around her shoulders. Not long enough to be feminine, so it just looks untidy.

Gone with the Wind – *I thought she would get bored half-way through. Even I get bored half-way through. There is only so far that silhouettes and sunsets can get you. But she went so quiet. Then when I approached the TV set to take the tape out at the half-way point, and suggest we go to the museum, she screamed. It was the loudest noise I had ever heard her make. She was usually so painfully shy. But she loved* Gone with the Wind *and I still don't understand why.*

Bookshopping is vital to my existence.

Not over the internet, that only works when you want something specific. Wandering around an actual bookshop you discover new things. Then you buy, or occasionally steal them, and they start becoming a part of you. Reading them and putting them on your shelves makes them fully a part of you. Re-read them and you renew the whole process.

I checked her social media again, because she's not answering her phone, so that is apparently the only way I am allowed to stay in contact with my own daughter. Only she hasn't updated her status for weeks now. There is a photo of her and some guy (he's not tagged in it), but apart from that. Nothing. For weeks.

I'm not sure what my options are now. I can't exactly just show up at her house.

I'm worried.

I do love her.

You know that, right?

It's almost two months since she posted on social media now.

I can't settle to anything but I desperately want something to do. My hands won't stop and I'm bouncing my leg against the sofa. I tried to watch a film but they all move too slow. I tried to listen to music but I had to keep skipping tracks.

Now I'm trying to write some pages or even single words for this novel but all I can write is this, describing the whole stupid thing rather than dealing with it.

I'm flapping about like an injured bird and all I can think to write is clichés.

Sometimes I feel like a bizarre new Tarot card. "The Scarred Woman." I wonder what I would predict if I was.

In this heat the scars on my arms glow purple. People get uncomfortable when I roll my sleeves up. I can tell by their body language. They suddenly get all stiff. It is useful when I don't want anyone to sit next to me on the bus though. No-one chooses to sit next to someone with two armfuls of scars.

Except guys with scar fetishes. I have dated a few of those in my time.

Does she have scars yet?

It's never going to be written. I think I've decided to give up. I might go back to painting instead. There is this little local gallery I could talk to. Most of the stuff they have in there is shite, so they should be happy to take mine on. And then they might sell. You can charge loads for a painting. In fact it looks better, it looks more professional if you charge loads.

I've got this tiny cut on my finger and it's bleeding everywhere. The blood that comes out of it is too red and thin to be real, until it dries and goes almost black. It's making everything I touch wet and slippery. I can barely hold this pen right now. It dries up, and then I bend or twist my finger the wrong way and blood starts pouring out again. I was going to cook tonight, I really was, but now I think I'm going to get a takeaway.

Definitely getting a kitten. They're more reliable than children. Then again, knowing my luck it would go out of its way to ignore me too.

She deleted me from her Facebook. That's why I haven't seen anything on there.

I don't think the phone number I have for her is accurate either. It's a landline. Who uses their landline any more?

All of this revelation is making me want to smoke.

I haven't felt like showering for a few days now. I can sense the smell growing on my skin but I can't bring myself to care about it. I doubt anyone will sit close to me. But I don't exactly want anyone to sit close to me right now.

Crème Eggs. I shouldn't eat the whole box, and I never set out intending to… But then I eat two and still fancy another one…and then in a box of five I have eaten over half so I may as well eat another one…and then there is only one left and I end up eating that one. This pattern happens several times every Easter.

The texture of words on paper. The bumps the pen makes on the page as it writes. The covering of pages in words. The layering of the pages. The way they turn more labouriously now that they are heavy with pen. Even though the movement of the pen can't actually add much weight.

This notebook was meant to be a novel, then a memoir, and now it seems to just be a journal. Yet I can't stop writing it. I keep getting the urge, whenever I think of something that makes sense, to write it down in here.

Futurama *is on the TV. I've been watching it for three hours now and I can't seem to move. I need the toilet but I just can't— I'm glad this notebook and my pen were on the arm of the sofa, right next to me.*

I just bought four pairs of identical jogging bottoms on Simply Be online. *Black, blue, maroon x 2. I can't be arsed to wear anything without a stretchy waistband.*

Today I'm going to go out.

I'm going to buy some books.

I like books.

I should go out.

Or I could order some on Amazon…

But I could browse in the actual bookshop…find something new…

But I could look at specific topics on Amazon. Something on Norse Mythology.

I'm going to do Amazon.

I've been watching Vikings. *I thought at first it was just a cheap* Game of Thrones *but now I've got into it. I much prefer American TV to British TV. Why does British TV in insist on endless crime dramas starring damaged detectives whilst there are such a variety of topics and avenues to be found in American TV?*

I like the stuff on Walter Presents too. Foreign language TV shows. Maybe just foreign TV in general is way more varied. And I'm not forgetting the period dramas with the plastic looking costumes, I loved

Merlin *and* Robin Hood *when mine was a kid, but they're stuck with a Sitcom structure. I suppose* Vikings *is very repetitive too.*

I'm not really writing, I'm just doodling with words. I'm not sure how it disintegrated to this point. Maybe I just never had anything.

I'm just playing about. Enjoying the sensation of drinking coffee in cafes and having something to do with my hands.

When I can be arsed to leave the house that is.

PART THREE

TILDA

If I don't let them in they've told me they have the authority to call the police. I've tried pretending to be asleep, but the threat remains the same, so in the end I always let them in. I open the door before they kick it down.

Once they're in, the first thing they always do is inspect the state of my flat. It's never the same people, but it's usually two nurses, or two support workers and one nurse. They start slowly walking round, staring at unwashed plates and making notes. They even check my toilet. They rarely make any comments out loud to me, they just write everything down.

Then they ask permission to sit down on my sofa, like that counteracts the invasion of privacy. I never say yes. They hover for a bit and then eventually they say "I'm just going to sit," and sit down anyway. I suppose if I complained about it they might get back up. I've never bothered to try it. I don't speak to them much, in the hope that they'll give up on me. Once the chemo made me throw up for a solid twenty minutes while they were there, and that made them leave early. Unfortunately the couple of times I've tried to repeat it they seemed to cotton on that I was faking it and didn't leave.

Every time that they come I convince myself I won't let them in. Every time I eventually do. It makes my skin crawl, the invasion. It's exactly like when they used to pierce my body with needles without my permission in the hospital.

I don't want to remember that.

Basically I'm stuck worrying about them coming until it next happens. They come every three days. So I have one day of relief, one day of worry and then the actual day. When it's the chemo week they miss a day, but apart from that there is no reprieve.

It's odd how different they are. The CPN is so cold, whilst the nurses on the Chemotherapy Suite will do anything for you. Even when they have to poke around to find a vein, they always ask permission before each new jab. It's bizarre that the two sets of nurses, the ones who come here and the ones I go to there, were probably on the same training course at some point.

MATILDA

1st January 2016

It happened.

I didn't

It was

When I think about it, I end up right back there.

Is that always going to happen?

Why do I sound so calm when I'm not?

When I can barely even—

I can't complete

Thoughts

I can't

I'm sorry. I'm not sure why I'm even…trying to

Writing this

I can't even finish sentences when I'm writing them down.

I need to

But it

I think I was

I think I was

I need to just write it but I can't

Can I really call it that

It

That word

Did that really happen to me?

Did it really happen to me?

I'm writing like I'm thinking because I need to get it out

I need to write the word down

The word

If I can't even

Do you think I should phone the police?

How am I so calm?

I'm too calm

Surely if what I think happened

Actually happened

If it actually happened

How can I be so calm?

So it can't have happened

Right?

Then how come I can remember it so

I can remember what his sweat smelt

And Lynx

I'm never going to be able to smell that again and not go back to

Writing stuff down is supposed to help. Why isn't this fucking helping?

MOTHER

I feel invaded.

Like I have pins and needles, but on the inside of my skin, inwards facing, long needles, pushing into my organs.

It started last night before I'd even started drinking wine, so it definitely wasn't that.

TILDA

I'm sure they did mention it to me, I'm not saying they didn't mention it to me. The doctors. Or a nurse.

I just mustn't have been listening to that bit.

I'm sure I would have agreed if I'd known, if I'd absorbed that piece of information properly.

At some point I must have said "No," to "Should we freeze your eggs?"

They must have asked me that question.

I mentioned it… at this morning's…after he told me the facts…and he said he thought he was the one who told me.

But I'm just one patient of hundreds, so maybe he can't remember it happening either. But it must have happened. They don't just…without asking…

I have only myself to be angry with.

In the thick of all that information I must have just tuned it out.

Once, when I was a teenager, a psychiatrist told me I shouldn't be having sex because having babies was too risky for Bipolar People. That's how he said it. "Bipolar People".

Was that message in my head when I failed to listen to the chemo side effects?

Fuck.

I suppose I can fuck all I like now, without the fear of—

It's not like I'd been planning—

I'm not someone who plans ahead.

I've never really thought about it properly.

Maybe I just assumed it was something for later on.

I'm not sure how much later on I was thinking. Not thinking.

Now there is no need…no point in thinking about it…and yet I'm thinking about it more now than I ever did when it was still a possibility.

I'm thinking of tiny hands, which grip tightly if you press your finger into the palm. A label is printed over the image, "I can't."

Today was the third day. They come round a couple of hours ago and nosed around my house. It's filthy. I don't care. They can do what they like to me.

Is this because of the kid and the pills?

Does the universe even work that way?

I don't think it does. How come so many rapists get away with it?

Maybe the universe only works that way for women.

By the way, the cancer is gone.

MATILDA

9th January 2016

Nothing happened.

I'm fine.

I can keep going.

Nothing.

"Nothing!" is what I end up shouting at Tom when he asks what's for dinner when I clearly laid out…

It wasn't anything.

I just see that situation…and cry…

I cried "Rape."

I don't cry rape because it didn't happen to me.

Not to me.

It really didn't happen to me.

I'd swear on that in court.

"Yes it is true. Nothing happened that night."

He didn't shove me against the sewing machine desk with the bulk of his body.

He didn't caress my face one moment, and clasp it tight the next. He didn't push me down so that I was laid out in front of him, ready for him to take what he wanted.

He didn't struggle to pull my pants down because I kept grabbing at his wrists.

He didn't then hold my hands on top of my stomach with

only one of his fists, whilst the other pulled down his jeans and boxers in one movement. Kick them away, so that he was half naked.

He didn't then hold both of my arms at my sides.

He didn't shove himself into a dry hole.

He didn't ram himself against, and in, me over and over.

He didn't shove his boxers in my mouth to stop me screaming.

I could breathe.

I didn't bleed.

I'm not still bleeding now.

MOTHER

I've got a UTI. Again. Acid wee. Its agony.

I keep trying to stop myself from going to the loo, but then it all saves up and I have a much longer wee when I do go. I'm not sure which is worse. Fewer trips with longer wee, or more trips with a shorter period of pain.

TILDA

I don't want to be writing this. I don't want to move at all. I want to be in bed, but since they're forcing me to sit here, I'd rather be still.

They used the spare key (which I stupidly keep under the mat) to come into my flat this morning, and demanded I got up. I hadn't let them in yesterday, but they didn't ring the police, they just came back with more staff today. If I stop writing, I'll have to answer their questions. I usually save this pad for poems. I could just be writing one word over and over and over and over and over but I need to look like I'm concentrating.

They're all just sat watching me. I suppose in professional circles it's called "Observing". I wonder what they'll write down about me today. Will they remark that I'm "unkempt", because I haven't washed, and my hairy legs are sticking out the bottom of my pyjamas?

I'm talking properly hairy, not just spikey. It stops me from fucking randomers if I have to shave in preparation.

Not that that matters. Not any more.

I could do—

Do you think they're going to take me back?

I don't want to go back.

I didn't realise that until I just thought, until I just pictured myself back on the ward. I didn't realise I cared that much.

I just had this really violent reaction to thinking about…it made me feel sick…it made acid rise in my throat.

They're still watching me. There's three of them. No doctors yet, but a Social Worker, a CPN and a student of some kind. They're probably waiting for the doctor to come. They need a doctor to make me—

If a doctor shows up he's going to sign off on me going back.

They can only do it for a few hours without one.

I wonder what they think I'm writing.

Maybe I should make notes on them, like they do on me.

Three women. One middle-aged, overly neat. One early twenties, overweight, doesn't want to be here. One nearing retirement, obsessive about blue clothes, hair unkempt.

One who claims to be a CPN just yawned.

Student keeps checking phone, Social Worker tries to stop her, student rolls eyes like teenager. Is student work experience? Surely they're too young at school? I must be low risk.

Golden oldie keeps curling her grey mane with her fingers.

…

…

I would keep making notes but to be honest there isn't much to say about these three.

MATILDA

1st February 2016

Tom keeps telling me to go out. I remember when he hated the thought of me going out. When I got that job, when I started the… He did nothing but complain.

If I stay in here with my books and my portable DVD player, I'm safe.

I don't need to be in the world to access the world. I can do it from here.

I have an imagination.

He gets the shopping so we're mostly eating tinned stuff. It's ok. I'm not all that hungry.

Last week he even asked me out to dinner.

I just couldn't. It probably would have been McDonalds anyway. I don't think I could stand the smell of chicken nuggets and slimy burgers right now. Even corned beef makes me sick into my mouth. I mostly eat tinned peaches. I like their sweetness and the sugar gives me energy quite quickly. I only eat a couple at a time though. It takes about a week to get through a whole tin.

He's even started cooking, lots of tinned curry. He sometimes waves it in front of me, as if ketchup-like, spicy sauce would tempt me in.

He just asked if I want to watch a film. Pointed at my Audrey Hepburn boxset. Seems he's up for something I like, rather than the action shit which he watches.

Should I say yes?

I know he'd watch maybe twenty minutes before getting fed up. I'd have to listen to him complaining that he's bored. He'd start his completely non-subtle suggestions that we should go upstairs and…

Shit.

No.

I can't…

I'm going upstairs by myself.

MOTHER

It's getting harder to hold myself together.

I watch TV programmes and picture myself as one of the characters for hours afterwards.

I'm obsessed with Elizabeth Moss. I walk around as Elizabeth Moss in Mad Men, *as Elizabeth Moss in* Top of the Lake, *as Elizabeth Moss in* The Handmaid's Tale. *I can feel her face as a mask. Not on top of my face, but instead of my face.*

I have her nose with the two kinks at the top, I open her eyes, I move her lips.

It's a flexible face. I can feel things in a more complex way through it.

I got rid of the UTI with some cream. Maybe it wasn't one in the first place. Just a stinging sensation. I couldn't face going to the doctor with it. I don't trust them.

TILDA

I'm still here. I'm still in my flat. They watched me for three hours, said something I didn't listen to, and then left.

Today I woke up and wrote four poems straight out.

Thinking about doing an online poetry course. The class is ok, but the tutor is pretty average. This online one is led by Francesca Simmons. I love her work. I won't get to meet her, but there are online video lessons and you can type questions and stuff.

The point is I got out of bed today and it is because of the poems and I want to develop that. I know I'm never going to make any money out of it. I just want to do it. It's something to obsess about that isn't harmful.

My ESA comes through tomorrow and I'm going to order poetry books with it. Not that many, they're really expensive, like a tenner each, but as many as possible, and then I'll just absorb it all and then—

I feel like I need to fill up and then use my pen to let it all out. Otherwise I'll just write about…it…about…all the shit that has happened.

Right now I feel like I'm running on

I feel empty. Nothing has gone from inside me…except the mass…my organs are all still there. The…equipment is still there.

But I feel like something has gone. I feel a gap. I wish it

ached. I wish it really fucking hurt. But it doesn't hurt. It's doesn't… anything.

I'm back to "Nothing" again.

A numb patch from the top of my pubes to my belly button.

If I prod it, I can't tell if the feeling is in the skin on my stomach, or the tip of my finger.

If I jab it with a pen I feel a dampened, slight pain, but nothing more.

It's like that whole area is dying off.

I tried to have a wank yesterday, and nothing felt good, so I just stopped.

I can't just sit here and poke at it. I know that now. I have poems to absorb. I have poems to write.

MOTHER

I'm not a real person.
Just fragments.
I don't know where any of these words are coming from.
They're not coming from me.

MATILDA

14th February 2016

He says he can't deal with me like this.

He can't deal with *me*. Has he really forgotten everything? How can he just say that? I did everything for him, and now when I'm…he says…

Fuck him.

All he does is game, and talk to fandom people in America.

I don't need him.

I don't need anything.

I don't deserve him.

I think he knows I fucked someone else.

I can't focus on anything. I can't even watch a film any more. I've ended up watching back episodes of *Nashville* because I can't think anything with a plot through. I don't even like country music.

I feel so sick all the time. As soon as I wake up I need to puke. I can't eat anything at all until mid-afternoon, usually later.

He still tries to make me eat when he cooks in the evening.

Sometimes I don't eat for days. The most I can do is five. Then I get too dizzy. I like the space of the dizzy feeling, but

I don't want to faint. It gets painful when I'm just puking up bile. When it gets to the point where there is blood, I drink tons of water so that I have something to come back up. It helps a bit, but it still hurts. The pain stops me admitting that it is my fault he is leaving. I don't have to think about that when it hurts.

I cheated on him and he can sense it. Every time I interact with him, he guesses another way I've betrayed him.

I don't deserve to eat. I don't deserve having him try to persuade me to eat. I don't deserve the food he's paid for.

I don't want to kill myself, but I hope I die.

No. It's more than that. All of this is because I deserve to die.

MOTHER

I think I've got a stomach bug. I feel all funny. Kind of light in the head, and then this morning I threw up, completely out of the blue. I hadn't eaten all that much the night before so it was mostly yellow sticky stuff with flecks of brown.

TILDA

I was trying to write fifty poems, because that's the usual number in the books of poems that I read; but apparently before you do a collection you have to do a pamphlet, which is only about fifteen to twenty. I reckon I can get that many together. It's a more realistic mission to focus on anyway. The tutor also said it's good to send out poems five at a time to literary magazines. This online course is much more focused on actually getting published, and I've decided that that is something I want to happen. If it doesn't I'll still have the poems for myself, but I really want it to actually happen.

I have twenty poems at the moment. Seven that I'm kind of happy with, four that I might consider sending out. I need to ask whether I send them all out to several magazines at once, or one magazine at a time and wait for responses in between. That could take ages. I'll check at the next video lesson.

I still go to the in-person workshops too, but all that is focused on the writing, not getting published. Which is good. To go to both classes. It's quite expensive, but I don't need much in the way of food. Learning from two people seems to be working well. Talking about all this only once a week wasn't enough, not when I'm writing so fast.

I've written loads more than twenty, but I chuck a lot of them. Sometimes the ones I write at the beginning of the week are so far from what I write at the end that they don't represent who I am any more, so I bin them. Maybe I've written another hundred that I've thrown away. I hate them so violently when I read them over again that I have to get rid of them.

I feel like I'm moving away from hospital and the sheltered shithole, and each poem takes me further away from them. They make it feel less like this is just a reprieve before I head on a road right back there again.

Thinking about it again, getting published doesn't matter all that much to me. As long as the poems are good. But getting published would be proof that the poems are good. It's all anyone on the online course talks about, so I feel like I should be doing it too.

I've been pretty aimless for a long time. Even before the hospital. The life with David wasn't really going anywhere.

I still think about that packet of pills sometimes.

It wasn't empty. I left a pill in there. I remember because I thought to myself before I took them, that four would be too many, that I should only take three. Then I put the packet down on the coffee table. The really low coffee table.

It's the one thing I will never write a poem about.

MOTHER

My brain won't stay in one place.

I can't do anything.

I've been eating tins of baked beans most meals. I have loads in the cupboard and I can't go out.

I tried. Yesterday, ormaybe the day before yesterday—

I stepped out the door and everything was so loud. So I went back inside again.

I'm looking into ordering my shopping online, but what if a man delivered it?

I suspect it probably would be a man. Maybe that's sexist.

The risk is too high.

So I'm eating baked beans.

I have eight tins left, so that's three weeks, just about…two and a half…maths isn't my strong suit and my brain just isn't obeying me right now.

MATILDA

23rd February 2016

I never used to cry. I've always found it very hard to cry; but the last few days, I can't stop.

I don't know why. I just can't keep it together.

Tom's the one who should be upset. He must know that I cheated on him. I never wanted to cheat on him. But it happened. Didn't it?

I fucking hate the position I've put him in. He's going to have to leave me, but I'm cruel and I don't want him to, so I've been clinging on. I haven't told him about that night…about how I led him on…about the time…about…

He saw the blood in the bed the next morning, but he just screwed up his face, the way he usually does when he sees evidence that I have periods. He didn't register that it was way too much blood for that.

I haven't had a period in a while. I think it must be the stress of the whole situation. All the lies. The mysterious crying. The way stupid things make me jump.

I jumped when Tom sneezed the other day. I never even used to jump at horror films.

Tom hates horrors. He hates most things I like. He watches his action films, plays endless games. Action is the one kind of film I don't like. Except maybe *Blade Runner*, at a push.

I'm fucking crying right now. I can't control it.

What the fuck happened to me?

Nothing.

I did this to myself.

I did tell him to stop.

I did—

But I should have tried harder…

I should never have gone back after the first… but I'd paid for the course in advance.

I should have shoved him off.

If I really hadn't wanted it to happen. I'd have…If I'd been…

It's like when parents suddenly have all the strength they need to lift cars to save their babies. If I'd objected enough that would have happened to me. I would have got more strength. I would have been able to shove him off.

But I didn't…

And now…

And now…

And now I…

I think I might be pregnant.

TILDA

Cancer isn't my life any more. As soon as possible psych services won't be part of my life any more; I'm going to do what they suggest for once. I cleaned the house, even did the dishes. And I've got something to fill the gap.

Things are going well. Things are actually going right. I can't believe it.

I get good feedback on most of my poems, from both courses. When I'm not writing poems I'm reading them. Books and pamphlets, but also stuff the other students on the courses have written. I make spidery notes on them all. People seem to actually like it when I give them comments. I think I sometimes have good ideas. It feels good to be wanted.

It also feels good to nurture something. None of the shit in my life goes away, but I can lock it into a different section of my brain.

All the good feelings, feel so odd. I call it good/odd.

EPILOGUE

MATILDA

7th June 2017

Hey there,

I know. It's been a while.

She's one year old.

I didn't buy the card. Tom must have.

It says "ONE YEAR OLD!!!" on it. It's pink. I'm not sure about the colour, or the triple exclamation marks. He said "Yeah but she loves it!!!" She doesn't love anything. She's a fucking baby.

She smiled last week. That's something I haven't even told Tom. He's been worried. Apparently an unsmiling baby is a bad thing. But I couldn't tell him. If I'd told him, he'd expect me to be excited about it. I would have to tell him that I didn't smile back.

Because I didn't.

I didn't smile back.

But I've decided I'm going to today.

Today I will smile at my baby.

I will.

I promise. I will.

Her name is Catherine.

Her face isn't Tom's face, but it isn't particularly…*his*… the father…the…I was going to say 'sperm donor', but what he did wasn't a donation.

She has my nose. She has my mother's eyes.

I phoned my mother the day she was born, but I didn't say anything. I know she's never going to be there for me. She has a life-long habit of standing me up, and then claiming I'm the one who ignores her.

But I just wanted a moment. A moment where there was a thread from Catherine, to me, to my mother.

She lied. Childbirth was fucking painful. No matter how you breathe. Tom is still trying to make up for the fact that I did it alone.

When he…that day…when he got sectioned again. I think the shock from that set the birth off early.

Don't worry. He knows it's not his. That's not an explosion waiting to happen. I couldn't leave that looming over us.

I expected her to be a noisy baby.

An angry baby.

And she isn't. I get told endlessly how lucky I am. She sleeps through the night. She only cries when she shits herself and she's sitting in it. I'm already looking into potty training her, I know it's a long shot, but I think she might be ready. I don't want to hold her back.

I wonder if he was a quiet baby.

Maybe he was quiet…and then something happened in his childhood that made him think that it was ok to…

Or maybe he just learnt it from porn.

I haven't smiled at her because, even though she doesn't look like him, she reminds me of something that was done to me. Because it was something that was done to me. It was not my fault.

But today I will smile at her.

Tom bought the card and a cuddly lion. So the smile will be my birthday present. Her first present from me.

MOTHER

This will be my last journal entry.

Writing isn't helping any more.

No, I don't mean that. I mean, it's not everything any more. It's not what I want to do any more. I might still write something, but I'm never going to write a book. It's taken me a couple of years to figure that out, but now I know it and I can move on from it.

I'm sure there are other things I can do.

I got this weird phone call last week. A number I didn't recognise. A heavy breather. Someone rang up and just breathed loudly down the phone at me. Usually I hang up straight away to that kind of thing; but that time I couldn't. For some reason I didn't want to.

It was whilst I was listening to that, the breathing, that I decided I want to be a counsellor.

Or a paramedic.

Or maybe a social worker.

Training to be a nurse would take too long, though maybe that would be a good ultimate aim.

I'm certain that this is what I want to do.

One of those four things.

TILDA

I'm still here.
    I'm still writing poems.

Thank you for listening to me, and reading the bits and pieces I wrote down in the moment.

But, if I can be blunt with you one last time: my life isn't poetic, and I'm not going to make up a poetic ending for you.

Acknowledgements

Thank you Mum, Dad and Henry for always supporting me, even when I'm being a (tiny) bit weird. I also want to thank Steve Dearden and The Writing Squad, for mentoring me; and Jenn Ashworth in particular- who supported me whilst I wrote the first draft of this book. Robert at Holland House Books- thank you for your sage editing advice and giving this book a home.

About the Author

Sarah is a multi-media writer and artist from the North-East of England. She makes work in a number of forms. She has previously published a book of poetry: *Voices*. She is currently developing a play about the history of women in film, with support from Arts Council England; and a piece of immersive artwork about Louise Bourgeois, with support from New Writing North. She is the author of many plays that look at both mental illness and feminism, including *Word Salad* which was performed as part of Alphabetti Theatre's award winning *The Rooms*. She is currently Associate Artist with Greyscale Theatre Company. Her work in film includes *Womb* – a piece about compulsive hoarding which was showcased by Channel 4.

She is publishing a children's book with Scholastic in 2020 and currently working on a novel about Georgina Houghton, and a non-fiction book about women film directors.